DARE TO FALL

FIREWEED HARBOR SERIES

J.H. CROIX

This is a work of fiction. Names, characters, businesses, places, events and incidents are either the products of the author's imagination or used in a fictitious manner. Any resemblance to actual persons, living or dead, or actual events is purely coincidental.

Cover design by Najla Qamber Designs

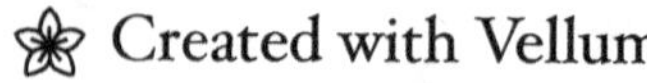 Created with Vellum

To new beginnings and family in all shapes and sizes.

Sign up for my newsletter for information on new releases & get a FREE copy of one of my books!

http://jhcroixauthor.com/subscribe/

Follow me!
jhcroix@jhcroix.com
https://amazon.com/author/jhcroix
https://www.bookbub.com/authors/j-h-croix
https://www.facebook.com/jhcroix
https://www.instagram.com/jhcroix/

Chapter One

FIONA

I tapped the button inside the elevator, and the doors began to close. Just then, I heard footsteps moving swiftly in the direction of the elevator. A hand shot out, catching the door, and a second later, a man appeared. My system felt jolted for one fiery second.

His eyes met mine as he smiled. "Made it." He stepped into the elevator, and the small space suddenly felt even more cramped. This man's presence and size filled it.

"Floor three?" he prompted when he glanced at the panel.

I cleared my throat with a nod.

"Well then, we're going to the same place."

He tapped the button, and the elevator

began to move before it abruptly stopped with an unsettling shake.

"Hm," the man said. "That didn't feel right."

"Did we stop on the wrong floor?" I asked needlessly because we'd barely moved.

"Something like that." He tapped the button again.

I looked around the small space, curling my arms around my waist and willing myself to stay calm. The man beside me pulled out a phone and tapped on the screen. A second later, he swore. Lowering the phone, he eyed his screen. "No reception." His gaze flicked to me.

Even though I could feel my heart racing and a sense of panic churning inside, I couldn't help but notice he had stunning eyes. They were a silvery shade of gray with thick dark golden lashes to match his hair, which was the color of burnished brass with glints of gold that shimmered even in the dim light of this elevator.

"We won't be here long," he assured me, his confidence belying the anxiety I felt.

"If you say so."

"I'm Blake," he offered after another moment. "There are only four stories, so we don't need to worry." His tone was light, and meanwhile, the space was feeling smaller and smaller.

When he arched a brow after several beats, I kicked my brain into gear. "Oh, I'm Fiona. Fiona Blake, actually."

He chuckled. "We share a name."

I smiled, thinking this man was way too handsome. Here we were, trapped in a tiny elevator, and my hormones were doing gymnastics at the sound of his rumbly laughter.

"It can't be too long," Blake offered another few minutes later.

He tapped the emergency button on the panel, only to get a crackling sound in reply. Suddenly, the elevator jerked, and I lost my balance, stumbling against him.

His arm curled around my shoulders as he steadied me. "That's a good sign."

"It is?"

"Sure. It means they're trying to work on it."

The elevator jolted again. Blake's arm hadn't left my shoulders, and it felt nice. He was warm and solid. Just when I started to feel hopeful, the elevator plunged. I cried out when it stopped with a shuddering thump.

"I think we just fell all the way down." My voice was a little shaky when I peered up at Blake.

He met my gaze, nodding. "I think so. That's either good or bad."

"Good?!" I squeaked.

"Good, because we can't fall any farther."

He slipped his phone out of his pocket again to peer at the screen. "Still no reception. What about your phone?"

I still had my purse looped over my shoulder, so I fished my phone out of it to glance at the screen. There wasn't a single bar of reception. "Nothing."

"Damn," he said slowly. "I guess we're here for a bit."

I took a breath, willing my heartbeat to slow. He leaned his hips against the wall, curling one hand on the railing. "Well then, tell me about yourself."

My eyes widened as I looked over at him. "Now?"

His lips kicked up at one corner, and my belly did a little shimmy. "We're stuck."

The elevator jerked again, really hard, and then lifted slightly. Once again, I stumbled into Blake, my purse falling off my shoulder and hitting the floor with a soft thump. My hand landed on his chest. I could feel the heat of him through his Henley shirt. I could also feel the muscled planes of his chest under my palm and the steady beat of his heart.

When I looked up at him, my heart drummed a little faster. We stared at each other.

"I want to call you Fi," he said, his slow and raspy voice sending heat pooling low in my belly.

"You can call me Fi," I whispered, a distant corner of my mind almost aghast that I hadn't leaped away from this man.

Maybe he wasn't a complete stranger, but all I knew was his name and that we were both trapped in a small elevator in an office building in Juneau, Alaska. I was here for an initial screening with a human resources department for a company for a new job in a smaller town nearby.

The elevator jerked hard and then abruptly started rising. I leaped back in a hurry, trying to catch my balance and failing when the elevator shuddered again.

Blake's hand landed on my hip as he steadied me. "I think we're moving up."

There was one more shudder before the elevator started moving smoothly, stopping when the lights indicated we were once again on the first floor. The doors opened just as I stepped away from Blake again.

"Not sure what went wrong, but we seem to have it working again," a man standing outside said. "For now, we're going to ask that you take the stairs."

I bent down to lift my purse, trying to gather my composure. Between being trapped in the elevator, my hormones coming out of a long hibernation, and telling a man he could call me Fi, I felt seriously flustered.

I straightened to find Blake's intent gaze on me. "Are you okay?" he asked, his tone low.

The man waiting outside the elevator was saying something to a woman who appeared.

"I'm fine," I said, mostly unsettled by the fact that I actually wanted to kiss this man in the elevator.

"Nice to meet you, Fi," he said, the heat banked in his eyes sending sparks leaping through me.

"You too, Blake."

He dipped his chin. "Take care then." He walked by, saying something to the woman standing outside the elevator. He appeared to know her. With a quick wave, he crossed over to a door and disappeared through it.

I glanced around until the man waiting said, "Stairs are right over there."

I followed where he pointed and hurried

up the stairs. A few minutes later, I twisted my hands together, waiting to meet with the woman doing my initial screening for a job interview. I needed this job. It was my ticket to a fresh start.

Chapter Two

BLAKE

A few weeks later

I looked over at Fiona Blake, trying to contain my body's reaction to her. She was sexy as fuck. With her brown hair with golden glints pulled back in a tight bun, almost severe. With her wide blue eyes and thick lashes. With her glasses she kept pushing up on her nose. She had sharp features—starkly angled cheekbones, a straight, narrow nose, and elegantly arched brows—all set off with the most kissable mouth I had *ever* laid eyes on.

I could *still* recall the feeling of her against me in that elevator. The soft give of her breasts against my chest when she stumbled and fell into me, the sweet curve of her hip, and the way my palm itched to slide over her bottom.

I never thought I'd lay eyes on this woman again, figuring it was just one of those brief encounters when you saw someone and wondered if it could be something other than two strangers crossing paths once. Here she was, interviewing for the chef position at my family's flagship winery, brewery, and restaurant. It was unsettling. I wouldn't technically be her boss, but my family owned the place.

I felt boxed in. David, the chef who'd worked for our family for over two decades, liked her. He was stepping down from being the main chef into a solely administrative role for the restaurant. He wanted us to hire Fiona, and I had no rational reason to refuse.

Chapter Three

FIONA

"Faster," David ordered.

I whipped through a series of tasks and plated the next dish, sliding it swiftly onto the shelf for the server to pick up.

"Faster," David ordered again as I moved at lightning speed to get the next order ready.

I was the new chef at Fireweed Winery in Fireweed Harbor, Alaska. David had been the only chef here before me. He was taciturn and direct. All in all, I supposed that was better than him being a straight-up asshole.

His most common order was "faster," followed by a clipped sigh. I was constantly biting my tongue and resisting the urge to be sly in return.

I didn't think that would go over too well with David. If he had a sense of humor, it only peeked out on occasion. None of his comments held even the slightest hint of sexual innuendo. That was a breath of fresh air.

The pace here was busy, really busy, but I loved it. It was precisely what I wanted. When I came to work, I put on my apron and dove into the day. The time flew until I finished. I still marveled that I was even here and had somehow scored this job even though I was pretty sure Blake Cannon, one of the owners who managed the winery and brewery, hadn't wanted to hire me. Every time I saw him, I couldn't forget the spark I'd felt between us in that brief encounter in the elevator in Juneau. I told myself it was pure coincidence that I'd ended up working in the place his family owned. There were times the world felt startlingly small. David liked me, sort of. Warm and fuzzy wasn't the description I would give David.

David was all business and very loyal to the Cannon family. Although I had only lived in Fireweed Harbor for a full two months now, I had quickly deduced the Cannon family was the equivalent of royalty in this town, complete with a messy past, some tragedy, and even some crime. David had explicitly ordered me not to get caught up in gossiping about the family. He said they had been through more than their share of pain and didn't need their employees falling into the "viper pit of gossip." His exact words.

I wasn't much of a gossip and had been burned by it more than enough in my own life. Not to say some of it wasn't deserved. My youthful indiscretions had been doozies. My hopes to find a fresh start far from those very indiscretions had led me here to this tiny town in Southeast Alaska.

By the time the dinner rush had quieted, it was almost ten o'clock. David looked over and gave me a firm nod. "Very good." At that, he turned and walked out of the kitchen toward the back.

Phil, one of the line cooks, cast me a grin. "Highest compliment."

I shrugged. "I'll take it." I checked the area where a row of tickets was usually lined up in front of the chef's station, realizing only one was left.

"You got that one?" I asked Phil and Tommy.

They nodded in unison. "We've got it. The magic hour has come, and you are done for the night," Tommy said.

"Thanks, guys," I called as I began tidying up.

"Hey," a voice said.

I glanced over to see McKenna Cannon walking into the back of the kitchen. I smiled over at her.

"Aren't you here a little late?" she asked when she stopped beside me.

I glanced at the clock. Shrugging, I looked back at her. "Not really. I stay until the rush is over."

She cast me a dimpled smile. "You're doing great. The reviews are raving."

"Reviews?" I yelped.

"I mean that in a metaphorical sense. Don't worry. Fireweed Harbor doesn't have official restaurant reviews."

I let out a breath. "Thank goodness. I'm not up for that."

She laughed softly, tapping her fingertips lightly on the stainless-steel counter across from me as she walked by. I finished tidying up and checked my prep for the following day before heading into the back where there was a break area. A row of lockers allowed the staff to tuck their jackets, purses, and the like as we came and went. David was long gone.

I shrugged out of my chef's jacket and

tossed it in the laundry basket before walking into the staff bathroom. After washing my hands, I splashed water on my cheeks. I threw my hairnet in the trash, looked at myself in the mirror, and dabbed a paper towel on my cheeks.

My blue eyes stood out against my olive-toned skin. I'd inherited my skin from my Italian mother and my eyes from my Irish father. I smiled at the thought of them. Different though they were, they were remarkably similar in personality, both passionate and boisterous. My father had passed away from cancer a few years after his diagnosis, and the ache of missing him was still sharp sometimes. My mother took care of him until the end.

I gave my head a little shake and finished drying my hands. When I walked out of the bathroom, Blake Cannon stood near the lockers, looking at something on his phone. That feeling I got whenever he was nearby shimmered to life inside. My hormones sure did like Blake. It was a pesky annoyance. Butterflies tickled my belly, and my pulse raced. Inconveniently, to get to my purse and jacket, I had to walk close to him.

When I cleared my throat audibly, he glanced up, his piercing gaze catching me instantly. Blake had dark blond hair and silvery-gray eyes. Of course, those eyes were nearly impossible to look away from whenever he looked at me. I felt as if I were caught in a tractor beam. I blinked, willing the heat rising in my cheeks to dissipate.

My shoes squeaked on the tile floor when I stopped a few feet away. "Hi." Even my voice squeaked. Ugh. I hated how uncomfortable I felt around Blake. He was one of the owners here, and I really needed this job.

"Hi. How did it go tonight?"

I'd seen Blake interact with others for two whole months now. Even with David, who didn't invite familiarity, he was easygoing and always quick to crack a joke. With me, there was an edge, something I didn't understand. That edge only fed into my insecurity around him. All the while, my hormones cheered and bounced for attention.

"Good." This time, my voice came out raspy. Fuck my life.

Blake nodded. "Feedback from customers is great, and David is happy with how things are working out."

"Is he? It's hard to tell. His most frequent suggestion is 'faster.'"

Blake stared at me for a beat before his

lips kicked up in a smile as he chuckled. "Ah."

My cheeks burned even hotter. I took a quick breath, willing my heartbeat to slow down. Taking a few steps, I reached for my jacket, slipping into it quickly. "Well, then," I said as I turned and looped my purse over my shoulder. "I'll see you tomorrow."

"That you will. Good night, Fiona."

Whenever he said my name, it sent shivers chasing over my skin. His voice was low and a little gruff.

"Good night, Blake."

I walked the few blocks home. Another bonus to this job was I didn't need a car all the time, which was good because I shared one with my mother.

I jogged up the steps to my apartment, which was on the upper floor of a small store. I felt like we'd scored the jackpot when we found this place because the rent was actually reasonable. I let myself in quietly and glanced over to find my mom sitting on the couch. She was watching some home sales show. She loved those.

"Hey, Mom," I said softly when she held her finger to her lips.

I shrugged out of my jacket and kicked off my shoes. I padded over to the couch, then leaned down and kissed my mom's cheek. "Is Lia asleep?"

"Of course," she whispered, giving me an absent-minded kiss on my cheek.

"Be right back."

I walked quietly across the living room and down the short hallway. By some miracle, we had three bedrooms. Two were tiny, and the other was just a tad larger. The biggest bedroom was my mother's. I wanted her to have more space. She'd tried to argue against it but finally caved, grumbling about how I was more stubborn than her.

My daughter's bedroom door was ajar, and I slipped into the room. She was sound asleep with her beloved stuffed dog hugged tightly in one arm. Rufus had been with her since she was a baby. He had spotted fur and floppy ears. His tail had gotten lost somewhere along the way in the six years since she'd had him. I brushed her hair away from her forehead, my lips curling in a smile. All of this was for her.

When I walked back out to the living room, my mother smiled over at me. "Show's over. How was work?"

I plunked down on the couch beside her. "Busy but I like it that way. How was Lia tonight?"

"You don't need to ask. She's always a good girl."

My mother always said that, but then my mother was patient and had a high tolerance for my eight-year-old daughter's bouncy and energetic personality.

"We're okay," my mother added softly when I met her gaze. She said that often.

I took a shaky breath. "We are."

Chapter Four

BLAKE

"I like her." David held my gaze with his firm tone, and I sensed he was almost daring me to question his judgment.

I didn't question his judgment. I liked Fiona as well, too much. She was a distraction, my delectable distraction.

"We're keeping her," David added.

"It's your call, David." I bit back a sigh.

He eyed me, pressing his tongue in the side of his cheek, something he did whenever he was about to tell me something I didn't want to hear.

"What is it?" I prompted.

"Do you like her?"

"Fiona is a perfectly nice person, an excellent chef, and a good employee. Of course, I like her."

"That's not what I'm talking about." A sly, knowing glint entered his gaze as he held mine.

I shrugged, annoyed with his perceptiveness. David had known me since I was a little boy and was a father figure to me in many ways. After my father passed, and our family had fallen into the misery of our abusive grandfather's presence in our lives, David had been a source of support for me. When I first took over management of the production for the brewery and winery, we had clashed. Not in any way that we couldn't have gotten past. But now, I recognized he had challenged me for a reason. He'd brought me up to scratch as a manager for this part of my family's business.

Honestly, I dreaded him ever choosing to retire from the restaurant fully. When he'd said he wanted to step back from the kitchen because his knees gave him trouble, I'd been beyond relieved when he'd insisted he keeps the reins of management for the restaurant. He was a fixture in my life and that of the rest of my family. We all loved him, and his steady, if bossy, presence was a salve to my emotional wounds.

As he studied me, his gaze sobered. "It's okay."

My throat felt tight. "What's okay?"

He gestured around my office. "Everyone here respects you. I loved your father, and I still love your mother. I hate that bullshit about a workplace being family because it usually means a toxic mess." His laugh was dry, and I couldn't help but chuckle. "It's never been like that for me with you all. You're my family. Because I was well-established here before your father passed away, your grandfather didn't mess with me. You all treat your staff very well, which is part of why you've been able to clean things up here. If I ever retire, it'll be okay."

My chest was really tight. He was voicing all the worries that had been swirling through my mind for months. David was the touchstone in this place. The winery and brewery made us far more money than this restaurant, but he was the axis in the wheel of all of it.

He was the first person I turned to when we tested something new. Gruff though he could be, he was kind underneath.

I took a quick breath, nodding. "I hope you're right."

"I am. With Fiona here, the restaurant will be just fine. She likes you too." I stared at him. "Hypothetically speaking." His lips quirked at the corners with that.

"If I like Fiona that way, it's a problem."

David shrugged. "Not really."

"What do you mean?" If I hadn't known I was crazy about Fiona yet, the fact that I was entertaining this conversation blared out warning bells.

"You manage the winery and brewery. The restaurant was a side project, to begin with. Maybe it's not the best idea to have the hots for her, but I'm her boss. Not you."

"Oh, for fuck's sake," I muttered.

"I just thought it might be useful for me to point that out." His gaze sobered. "I don't know how much you know about her, but she really needs to keep this job."

"What are you talking about? Most people want to keep their jobs. What's different for her?"

"She has a daughter, you know."

"I didn't know that." My curiosity was piqued.

"I thought not. Fiona's making some changes to the menu. I'm also going to make it clear to the staff that she's in charge of the kitchen now. They can consider me her assistant."

My mouth dropped open as I stared at him. "What?"

David cracked a rare wide smile. "I thought you'd like that. I can't handle the full-time pace of being the lead chef. I can handle the management and helping her out in a pinch. Being on my feet less will be fucking fantastic."

David had started working for us when he was twenty years old, back when the restaurant was a side project.

"I'm Fi's boss—" He began.

I cut in. "Since when does she go by Fi?" It shouldn't have bothered me, but my brief interaction with her in that elevator elicited this sense of possessiveness around that nickname. I hadn't heard anyone else call her that.

David shrugged. "I don't know. I call her that sometimes. Her mother does too."

"Her mom?"

"Yeah. You don't know much about her, do you? She rented an apartment from Fireweed Property Management, you know, your family's company," he said with a brow hitch. "It's her, her mom, and her daughter. When she moved to town, I connected her with McKenna, like we do for any new staff who don't have a place to live. She set Fiona up with the property management company."

"Hmm." I tried to sound bland when what I wanted was to ask a few hundred more questions about Fiona.

Blessedly, David left when he got a phone call. Restless, I stood from my desk and walked out. Whenever I was at loose ends, I usually did a loop through the whole place.

I passed through the brewery area, checking on a few of the tanks and the status of our production. I made it through the kitchen, experiencing a shaft of disappointment when I didn't see Fiona busy at the stove. Of course, I shouldn't even be wondering where she specifically was, but I *was*. I was acutely aware of her presence, or lack thereof, whenever she was supposed to be here.

The last place I checked was the staff break room. That was where I found her. Even though I told myself I wasn't looking for her.

She was on her phone, her shoulder resting against the wall beside the row of lockers. Her head was tucked down, and her brow furrowed with worry. "Okay, okay. I'll try to get there as soon as I can." She lowered the phone, staring down at it.

"Is everything okay?" I asked as I approached her.

Fiona's head whipped up. I took the moment to study her as she stared back at me. Her beauty was quiet, it almost felt a little hidden. She always kept her glossy hair pulled back in a bun. Her eyes stood out, sapphire blue with thick lashes. Her skin was a subtle olive color, warm and inviting a touch. She always dressed modestly in blouses that buttoned all the way up and skirts that fell below her knees. She couldn't hide her curves, but I sensed she tried.

She blinked quickly, looking down at her phone. "My daughter is sick at school, and I need to pick her up. I don't have my car. I need to call my mom and—"

I cut in. "I can take you."

Her gaze whipped back to mine, her brows flying toward her hairline. "You would do that?" Her voice squeaked at the end.

"Of course." I glanced at my watch. "Will you need to take the rest of the day off?"

She shook her head quickly. "My mom is home. She'll take care of her."

"Get your things. I'll go let the line cooks know."

I didn't wait for her reply and spun around, striding briskly out of the break room and toward the kitchen. My eyes landed on Tommy, one of the line cooks. "Fiona has to run out to pick up her daughter from school. She'll be back in thirty minutes."

Tommy nodded, calling, "Got it!"

She'd probably be back sooner, but I figured that gave her a cushion. Only moments later, we were driving toward the elementary school.

I slid my eyes sideways. Fiona sat quietly, her gaze angled slightly toward the window and her hands laced together in her lap. Her nose turned up at the end, and her cheekbones were angled high on her face, setting off her mouth. Her bottom lip was *so* kissable. Even now, just riding in the truck, I wanted to lean over and turn her face toward me and kiss her, all so I could feel her plump lips.

"You said the elementary school." I forced myself to look ahead. "What grade is your daughter in?"

"First grade." Fiona glanced at me quickly, and our eyes collided before we both looked ahead again.

"What's her name?"

"Lia. She's named after my mother, Natalie. She goes by Lia."

"Pretty name." Our eyes met again, and it felt like flint striking stone with sparks leaping in the air between us.

"David told me he's happy with how you're doing," I offered, trying to find something to talk about. "It's good for him to shift solely to focus on management. He's had some knee issues."

She was quiet for a beat. "He's never mentioned it, but I can tell it's hard for him to be on his feet. I mean, you're on your feet a lot, but—"

I interjected. "I'm certainly not on my feet as much as anybody is in the kitchen. As far as I can tell from the time you arrive until the time you leave, you're on the move in there," I pointed out dryly.

Fiona laughed, and I tried to remember if I'd heard her laugh yet. Her low and throaty laughter sent fire sizzling through my veins.

"I suppose so."

"I'm glad you and David get along."

"He intimidated me at first, but he's a softy. I figured that out," she said.

My heart tumbled in my chest when I glanced her way and collided with the twinkle in her eyes.

Fuck me. It wasn't just the chemistry with Fiona. There was something else there, something I didn't usually feel. Honestly, something I'd never felt. I wanted to *know* this woman, to unravel the layers she kept wrapped tightly around her.

I forced my attention to the conversation. "David *is* a softy. Sometimes it takes a while to see it."

Just then, I saw the sign for the elementary school and slowed to turn onto the road. A moment later, I pulled up in front. "Where should I park?"

She gestured toward the circle that curved in front of the main entrance. "Just wait there. I already texted to let them know I was on my way."

Once I came to a complete stop, Fiona slipped out and jogged into the school. A few moments later, she returned with a little girl walking at her side. They held hands, and her daughter was looking up and saying something.

Fiona opened the back door, gesturing inside. "Hop in."

Her daughter climbed in, immediately buckling her seat belt.

"I'm supposed to be in a booster," she announced.

"I'm sorry, I don't have a booster," I said.

"That's what Mama said." Her eyes held mine. "I'm Lia."

"Very nice to meet you, Lia. I'm Blake."

"That's my last name!"

Fiona cast me a quick smile. She glanced back at her daughter. "Blake can be a first name and a last name."

Fiona quickly explained that Lia had felt sick after lunch but was feeling better now. "My guess is she ate too much," she added.

Lia chimed in, "I had too much milk."

Fiona asked Lia a few questions about school while I marveled at how startlingly alike they looked, both with glossy hair and warm olive skin with a rosy hue.

"How are you feeling now?" Fiona asked just as I slowed to turn into where she directed me.

Lia let out a little sigh. "My tummy still feels funny, but I don't want to throw up anymore."

"Well, you'll spend the afternoon with Gigi."

When I glanced toward Fiona, she added, "Gigi is my mom. Lia started calling her that when she was little, and the name stuck."

Once I parked, Fiona hopped out and helped her daughter out of the truck. Lia turned back, waving. "Bye!"

"Bye!" I returned with a quick wave and a grin.

I watched as they walked up the stairs to the upper floor. Questions tumbled through my thoughts. Where was Lia's father? How did they end up here in Fireweed Harbor? And why?

A moment later, Fiona hurried down the stairs. She was inside my truck in a flash. "Sorry if that took too long," she said breathlessly.

"You didn't have to run. It's no big deal."

She looked over at me. "You're doing me a favor, and I'm supposed to be at work."

"It's really no problem."

"Normally, we have a car, but it's in the shop for an expensive repair. I have to budget before I can get it fixed."

"What is it?"

"Brakes and tires. You know how Alaska doesn't have inspections?"

"Oh, I do. Not really the best plan, all things considered," I offered dryly.

"The mechanic told me I could skate by with my tires, but he recommended replacing them. He was worried enough about my brakes that he didn't even want me to take it from the shop."

As I was backing out, I spoke before considering it. "I can fix your brakes. And if you get the tires, I'll put them on for you."

Fiona whipped her gaze toward mine as I began to drive forward. "What?"

"I love working on cars. Just something I do on the side. We have a garage on-site for our property management company. During the winter, we maintain the parking lots and so on. It's more affordable to take care of vehicle maintenance ourselves."

I stopped before turning onto the road. She studied me, her eyes narrowing. "Are you sure?"

"Absolutely. You need a car."

Fiona's cheeks flushed pink. "I bet you think it's ridiculous that I have to budget for this."

"Not at all. It's called life. After you're done at work today, I'll drive you down to the shop, and you can pick up your car and get the tires. You can throw them in the back of my truck." I thumbed over my shoulder. "I'll take care of it over the weekend."

"Wow. Thank you."

"Anytime."

When we got back to the winery, I walked beside her and held the door open at the employee entrance. She slipped by me quickly. My eyes were drawn to watch the subtle swing of her hips. My body tightened.

She wasn't the only employee I'd ever offered to help with their car. But I knew maybe it wasn't the best plan. Spending time with Fiona outside of work was risky.

Chapter Five

FIONA

I was relieved the afternoon was busy at work. I always preferred to be busy so I didn't track the clock. In this case, I didn't want to dwell on Blake. His offer to help with my car was incredibly kind and very needed. Between the brakes and the tires, it was going to be almost two months before I could save up the money. This way, I could just put the tires on my credit card and pay it off.

I didn't need to dwell on the hot, sexy Blake. And just because he offered to help with my car didn't mean he was actually nice.

Blake hasn't done anything to lead you to think he's a jerk.

Maybe not, but you didn't exactly notice what Johnny was doing before it was too late.

As soon as I thought about my ex, my cheeks heated. The embarrassment I still felt whenever I thought about the mess of my life and just how bad it could've gotten clung to me like gum on the bottom of a shoe.

Johnny wasn't all bad.

No, but he left you a mess to clean up.

I kept waiting for the day when I could give myself some grace for my adolescent regrets. I had fallen in love with Johnny Kingston.

He'd had a sly sense of humor and an underlying sweetness that had seemed irresistible when I was sixteen. I hadn't known he was also the primary dealer of stimulants in our high school in Seattle. By the time I was pregnant, he was dealing more than that, and I didn't even know. When I found out, we broke up. When Lia was four, he'd died of an overdose in a bar. I didn't know who to trust and was mortified to tell my parents what had happened. I'd also been broke and barely getting by. Johnny had always helped with money, and I hadn't even known how tainted it was.

I'd gone to food banks for weeks and

stayed in a homeless shelter until I swallowed my pride and called my mother. I blinked at the sudden rush of tears to my eyes. We were safe now. When I came to Fireweed Harbor, I just wanted to escape the mess of my life. I'd had a job in a small restaurant in downtown Seattle, making decent money as a line cook. My boss, a seriously good chef, told me about the chef job here in Fireweed Harbor because he thought I had a lot of potential.

I'd taken what little savings I'd scraped up and packed my mom and Lia onto the ferry with my old car. I'd been naive, not realizing how remote this area was. To this day, I felt so lucky I'd gotten the job.

"Fiona!" Tommy called.

His voice snapped into my anxiety-filled walk down memory lane, and I lifted my gaze. He waggled his eyebrows dramatically. "The salmon special?"

"Oh!" Blessedly, my hands had been moving all along. My muscle memory had me flipping the salmon as I seared it quickly on the stove.

Stay focused, I ordered myself.

When the evening ended, I checked with David before I left. "Good for me to go?" I asked.

He glanced up. "Of course."

I kept expecting something to go wrong here, but then my life had been skating on the edge of disaster once I got pregnant in high school.

"Thank you," I replied.

He was already reading something on his laptop, calling in reply, "See you tomorrow."

I hurried into the break room, which was bustling with employees. This was the in-between time when the early crew swapped out with the afternoon and evening.

I liked the comfortable vibe here. The restaurant industry was notorious for grueling hours and not the greatest pay. You couldn't work for hours on your feet in a fast-paced restaurant without getting tired, but we all started and stopped when we were supposed to. They actually paid overtime here, and I still marveled at that.

I supposed when a multinational corporation made the kind of money they did, it only made sense for them to do that. I was bound and determined to make it work here.

Blake and I hadn't discussed how to handle this thing where he drove me to pick up my car. I wondered if I should walk to meet him there.

Just as I was worrying over this, he appeared in the back area, casting me a quick smile. "I'll give you that ride." He turned to say something to Joan, an older woman who helped out in the kitchen. She nodded, sliding her arms into her jacket and reaching for her purse out of the locker before they walked over to me.

Joan smiled at me. "I hear we're both getting a ride. Blake is dropping me off at my daughter's house. I'm babysitting for her this evening."

I was simultaneously relieved and disappointed. Relieved because having Joan with us removed the awkwardness of me leaving with Blake. Disappointed because a part of me craved time alone with him. That wasn't smart, not even a little.

"Oh, great," I said with a smile. "He's taking me to drop my car off for new tires and brakes."

Blake smiled at us, his gaze holding mine for a moment. "Are you ready?"

"Just a sec." I quickly slipped into my jacket and grabbed my purse.

A moment later, we walked out together. I stayed a few steps behind Joan, thinking I would follow her lead.

When we reached Blake's truck, he

opened the passenger door. "You ride in the front," Joan said. "I'm first on the way."

I climbed in, acutely aware of where my shoulder brushed against Blake's chest when I stepped past him. Once we were all inside and Blake was driving down Main Street, I glanced back toward Joan. "That's nice you can help with babysitting. I don't know what I would do without my mother's help."

She smiled. "I love it. Many clichés are not true, but the one where being a grand-parent is more fun than parenting is very true. I get a lot more sleep than I did when my kids were little." She chuckled.

"Sleep for the win," I teased.

We passed through the business area of downtown Fireweed Harbor, transitioning into an area with a mix of cute little houses before Blake pulled over to the side of the street and parked. "Give me a sec," he began. "I'll get —"

Joan rolled her eyes, already unbuckling her seat belt and opening the door. "Blake, it's very sweet that you want to get the door for me, but entirely unnecessary." She looked back toward me. "I used to babysit for this man. That's why he has such good manners. His mother gets plenty of credit, but I helped."

Blake smiled affectionately at her. "You do. Have a good evening," he said as she closed the door.

Once Joan disappeared out of sight through the front doorway of a small home, Blake's voice reached me. "Let's go pick up your car. Do you have a tire preference?"

He began driving, turning down a side street to turn back around and travel through town. I glanced at him when he came to the stop sign. A little jolt of electricity sizzled through me when our eyes met. "Uh, no. I don't really have any preferences. Do you have any recommendations?"

"You'll want to get all-weather tires, potentially something with studs for the winter."

"Studs?"

He flashed me a smile. "Little steel studs in the tires. Many people have both winter and summer tires in Alaska."

The idea of purchasing two sets of tires was well beyond my budget. "I don't drive that much," I said quickly. "You saw where I live. I usually walk to work. My mom and I share the car, so she uses it for errands and work."

He held my gaze for a beat before

glancing ahead and turning onto the road. "I would recommend all-weather tires."

He drove along, and the space inside his SUV felt tiny. Heat shimmered through me. I didn't need to be getting all hot and flustered over one of the restaurant's owners. Maybe David was my boss, but even worrying over that detail felt like splitting hairs.

There was that, and Blake was so far out of my league that it was a joke to even consider otherwise.

In short order, we arrived at the mechanic shop. Although it was late evening, it was still open. I had already learned with the long summer evenings here, many places had extended hours. Everyone there appeared to know Blake. He helped me choose a set of tires. In reality, it was all about how much I could afford, but I was grateful for his guidance.

I followed him from there to the vehicle storage and garage. It was a ways out of downtown Fireweed Harbor, off a side road in an industrial-looking area. There appeared to be a small airport with a row of planes tethered in place. I had already become familiar with the sight of small planes crisscrossing the sky above town.

Blake turned into a parking area just beyond the airport behind a large steel building. He gestured out of his window for me to follow him into the garage, which was huge. Several vehicles were parked inside along the row of garage doors. Blake pulled over to the side, waving for me to pull past him. I came to a stop and cut my engine, feeling unaccountably nervous.

Chapter Six

FIONA

I glanced around my car. Lia had named my little gray hatchback Chipmunk because there used to be a squeaky door. This car had served me well. She was reliable and mostly low maintenance. The back seat was a typical back seat for a single mom. A few toys and my daughter's favorite drawing book were scattered on the seat. I let out a soft sigh. Cleaning my car fell on the list of things I never found the time to do.

I hadn't realized Blake was waiting outside the driver's side door for me. When I looked up, I let out a startled squeak. My disobedient pulse kicked a little faster. His lips curled at the corners, sending butterflies into a mad spin inside my belly.

I took a quick breath, once again questioning the wisdom of taking Blake up on his offer. I tried to tell myself I saw him almost daily at work anyway. At this point, trying to back out of this would only create more awkwardness.

I grabbed my purse and climbed out of the car quickly. When I shut the door, I took a step back, instantly bumping into it.

Blake's assessing gaze coasted over my face. "I should be able to take care of your brakes over the weekend. Will that be okay?"

I swallowed and nodded quickly. "Of course. That's faster than they were going to be able to do it anyway. They said it would be two weeks."

"They tend to be busy."

I bit my bottom lip, willing the heat rising in my cheeks to dissipate while knowing it was a futile effort. Nervous, I licked my lips. "Thank you for offering to do this. I know, maybe money isn't something you worry about, but for me, this helps a lot."

He was quiet for a beat. "My family may own Fireweed Industries, but we're pretty down to earth. It all started with the winery and restaurant."

I tried to take a breath, but I could barely get any air in my lungs. My pulse galloped along, leaving me breathless as heat suffused my body.

Blake's eyes darkened as he stared at me. The air around us felt weighted with a charge about to go off.

"Fiona—" He began just as he took a step closer to me.

I hadn't thought it possible for my heart to beat faster, but it did, casting out beats recklessly, stumbling and tripping over itself. All the while, that incessant attraction I felt for him rose swiftly inside. Liquid need spun through my veins, sending sparks scattering as heat pooled low in my belly.

"What is it?" I rasped.

My mouth went dry at the intent look in his eyes. I saw the answering flare of desire, flickers of need banked in his gaze like hot embers.

This, this part of me I tried so hard to keep buttoned up, buried behind my hair pulled back tightly, behind my clothes neat and tidy. Because this side of me, reckless and craving release, was what had brought so much trouble before.

As I stared deep into Blake's eyes, I didn't care. I just wanted to *feel* again. He called to that part of me, catching the binding I had wrapped around my passion, around my heart, and unraveling it with nothing more than a look.

He took another step closer. He was right there in front of me. There was nowhere for me to go, not that I wanted to go anywhere. I craved the feel of his power, the potency of his presence.

"Fi." His low and velvety voice sent a frisson of awareness down my spine.

When he used that nickname, my mind flashed to our brief encounter in the elevator when I never imagined I'd see him again. I felt my core clench, and I had to rub my thighs together, so swift was my arousal.

He moved slowly, almost as if he expected me to bolt. All the while, I was nearly vibrating from the force of my need, from how desperately I wanted him to kiss me.

Lifting a hand, he trailed his knuckles along the edge of my jaw. Breathless, I quivered as his touch slipped down the side of my neck where my pulse tapped out a rapid, staccato beat, wild and trampling.

"Can I kiss you?"

Chapter Seven

BLAKE

10 seconds earlier

Fiona's eyes were wide, the blue darkening almost to navy as she stared back at me, never once looking away. My heartbeat echoed in a thundering drumroll, need a sharp ache inside. I had just now touched her, nothing more than a brush of my knuckles along her silky soft skin. My cock was so hard I could feel the press of my zipper against it.

Her tongue darted out, sliding across her bottom lip as we stared at each other. She blinked.

"Yes." Her voice was a low, throaty rasp.

I hadn't known it was possible for my cock to get even harder. Need sizzled down my spine, and heat blazed through me. It felt as if the very air around us was snapping and crackling with sparks.

I moved slowly, realizing this moment was like nothing I had ever experienced. I'd had my share of fun and enjoyed sex as much as any guy, but this was something else, something deeper. The very act of standing before Fiona with my knuckles resting along her collarbone held me fast. I could feel the press of her nipples, taut peaks against my chest. With my arousal nestled against the soft curve of her belly, I knew she could feel my hot, hard length, swollen to the point of aching.

Usually, sex was fun, almost light. Yet this was a bone-deep need, the force of it knocking me off balance internally.

I shifted incrementally closer, and her hips rocked against me. I felt her move slightly, and she rubbed her thighs together. I knew, I just *knew*, if I tugged her prim skirt up that I would find her wet.

The mere thought of that sent a shot of blood straight to my cock. I nudged against her. She bit her lip, letting out a little whimper, and the sound galvanized me. I dipped my head, whispering, "Okay then," against her lips just before I pressed my mouth to hers.

Her lips were soft and plump and warm. For a moment, I held still, my mouth lingering, before drawing back. Her eyes were wide pools of desire, and she whimpered again.

I reached up, my fingers sliding through the elastic that held her hair in a tight ponytail. "Can I take this out?"

She nodded. Another moment later, I dragged that elastic loose, and her glorious hair fell around her shoulders. Sweet fucking hell. She looked downright wanton with her hair down. It was no wonder she kept it up. If I'd seen it down sooner, I probably would've dragged her into my office, bent her over, and fucked her from behind.

I promised myself I would do that at some point in the not-too-distant future.

"Fuck, Fiona," I rasped. "You are the sexiest fucking woman I've ever seen."

Her cheeks flushed a deep shade of pink. Then I was kissing her again, this time claiming her mouth, devouring it, as her tongue glided against mine. Our kiss was downright carnal. I couldn't get enough of her. She tasted sweet, a little bit like sugar, and she smelled the same. I wanted to unwrap her and taste every inch of her skin.

Our kiss went on and on while our hips rocked together. She made these little sounds in the back of her throat that drove me wild.

At some point we broke apart, both desperate for air. As much as I wanted her more than air, I did have to breathe. We stared at each other, the sound of our ragged breathing surrounding us.

"Tell me something," I said when I could manage to speak.

"Anything."

"Are you wet?"

She bit her lip, nodding just once.

"Can I touch you?"

Chapter Eight

FIONA

I could barely think with need rampaging through me and holding me in its grip. I was utterly at Blake's mercy and would do anything he asked.

When he asked, *"Can I touch you?"*

There was only one answer.

"Yes," I whispered.

I could feel my heartbeat in my pussy, and I was drenched, soaked with need for him, *only* him.

He barely shifted away from me, and even that made me feel a little bereft. I had been grinding against the hard ridge of his cock, experiencing little jolts of pleasure. I usually wore demure skirts that fell below my knees. I found them more comfortable at work with long days on my feet. His hand curled over the hem as he slid it up slowly, and I shivered at the brush of his knuckles on my thigh.

Cool air struck my skin. His eyes held mine as I felt his palm slide up the inside of one thigh, the calloused surface of his touch sending sparks leaping across my skin. I let out a whimper when he cupped his palm over my mound, his fingers pressing against the wet silk.

"Oh, sweetheart. You are so very wet."

I nodded and swallowed. Oh. My. God. I was agreeing with this man about the state of my arousal.

He hooked a finger on the edge of my panties, pushing them out of the way. My head fell back with a groan when his fingers slid through my swollen, slippery wet folds.

"Look at me," he ordered.

I did as he commanded, holding his gaze through heavy-lidded eyes as he sank two fingers inside me.

"Come for me."

That was all he had to say as his thumb teased over my swollen clit. I did as he demanded, pleasure exploding through me as I came in a noisy burst, my pussy clamping down around his fingers. I couldn't look away from him. He watched the whole time as I came apart after nothing more than two strokes of his fingers inside me.

My head fell back again as I caught my breath, pleasure ricocheting through me.

"Oh my God," I whispered as I stared at him.

His fingers were still buried inside me. He looked as shocked as I felt.

Chapter Nine

BLAKE

Later that night, I sat at my kitchen table, idly tracing my fingertips in a circle around an empty bottle of beer.

I'd been so wound tight when I got home after dropping Fiona off that I'd taken a shower, finding a quick release by my own hand. Fuck me. I still couldn't get the sight of Fiona coming apart in my arms out of my thoughts.

She had been, simply put, stunning. My mind flashed back to the first time I saw her in that small elevator, before I knew she would cross my path again. Her hair had been pulled back tightly and twisted into a bun like it usually was. I mentally traced her sharp features—angled cheekbones, a narrow nose, and those boldly arched brows. Her mouth was something else. She couldn't do anything to hide those lush, perfectly kissable lips. There was also the way her nose tipped up just a little bit at the end. Almost as if it was bucking her effort to make herself look severe and tidy.

With a mouth like that, she was pure sin. Witnessing her guards fall away had nearly brought me to my knees. My cock twitched just now thinking about it. I let out a groan as I leaned back in my chair, glancing out the windows into the darkness.

I had built my own place with the help of a contractor and my brothers. It was small, but exactly what I needed. The curved crescent of the moon rose in the sky, casting a shimmer on the water of the harbor. Close to downtown, I was just past the busy area, where I could have enough acreage for some privacy, but it was still convenient.

There were those in Alaska who wanted to get as far away as possible from anything that could be confused with civilization. I personally liked heat, hot water, a grocery store right down the street, and a job that I could get to within a few minutes.

My eyes arced about my kitchen. Slate tiles in a soft gray were on the floor with a small island in the center and counters flanking two walls. The table was situated by the windows. The tile shifted to hardwood flooring in the living room area, creating a natural divider between the spaces. My living room had a vaulted ceiling with windows from top to bottom, offering an even better view of the harbor than my kitchen had. There was a bathroom with laundry and a back entrance with a mudroom, a necessity in Alaska during the messy winter and spring seasons.

Stairs off to the side of the living room led up to a balcony. Up there were the main bedroom and main bath, along with a guest room and another bathroom. Hypothetically, I could expand and add more bedrooms to make it more appealing if I ever chose to sell. Yet I always imagined it would just be me.

I loved my family dearly. Growing up in a household with seven siblings was busy. Even though we had painfully lost one, we were still more than a volleyball team. That was the joke among us when we were kids.

I took a breath, my mind spinning back over these past six months or so. I'd thrown myself into work, focusing on expanding our production of wine, beer, and mead. Ever since we had learned we had a nephew, the

son of my eldest brother who'd died of alcohol poisoning a month before he was due
to graduate from college, old feelings that I'd
tried to stuff deep inside kept kicking up.

I loved my mom, and I missed my father
who'd died when I was young. As much as I
missed my father, I held a stone of resent-
ment heavy in my heart. Because if our dad
hadn't died, our grandfather never would've
stepped in to help, and he never would've
been the destructive force in our family. He
had a terrible temper and lashed out at all of
us verbally. Jake and Rhys occasionally took
the brunt of his hand when he hauled off and
slapped them hard enough to knock them
over.

He never touched any of the other of us,
not that I knew of. It had only been a year or
so before our nephew came blasting into our
lives that we learned our grandfather had
raped Jake. No one knew if it happened more
than one time. Our cousin had witnessed it,
and he carried that secret with him for so
many years that he had panic attacks.

Archer now lived in Willow Brook,
Alaska, heading up one branch of Fireweed
Industries. He had shut down a mining operation and turned it into a renewable energy
manufacturing business. He was in love and

happily married now. Rhys was doing better now too. He and I were tight, and for that, I was grateful. I hadn't realized how much I'd kept bottled up with the events of the last two years.

This entire train of thought was kicked up like a hornet's nest by Fiona. Pretty Fiona, who kissed like a dream and came all over my fingers.

It wasn't just the chemistry that blazed between us. It was the way I felt when I looked in her eyes and her guard fell. Something latched on inside me. I felt vulnerable.

It was complicated enough to be in lust with Fiona and decidedly more complicated to sense myself wanting more from her. I didn't allow myself to feel vulnerable. *Ever.* Everyone knew me as the easygoing one in our family, and I liked it that way. Rhys had been thrust into being the oldest sibling after Jake died, and he took it seriously. He always made sure we were taken care of one way or another. Whether it was work, money, or whatever, he was there.

I knew how much it weighed on him that Wyatt, one of our younger brothers, kept his distance, refusing to even work in the family business. Wyatt's twin, Griffin, didn't work in the family business, either, but he didn't keep us at arm's length the way Wyatt did.

Adam and Kenan were a pair, naturally, because they were also twins. Adam was the more serious one, the numbers one in our family. He had been a natural fit to take over as the CFO for the corporation once Rhys needed him. Kenan was sort of the everything guy. He did whatever was needed. He helped out at the winery, took off to handle pesky HR issues, and so on.

McKenna was the only girl in our family, so that alone made her stand out. She handled public relations with flair and ease. She was guarded and kept herself emotionally buttoned up, but it made sense. Her high school boyfriend had screwed her over so bad it's a good thing he moved because we'd have collectively kicked his ass. She still got embarrassed if it came up.

Griffin and Wyatt were both hotshot firefighters. Griffin was the only one Wyatt was really close to, and he protected Wyatt's choice to keep his distance. I had so many questions about it and hoped someday I'd understand. Hotshot firefighting suited them. They were both risk-takers.

That left me. I was the one who smoothed everything over, the one who never tried to cause any trouble. I was a natural fit to run the winery. I loved it, I truly did, but I also knew why everyone expected me to. I was the social one, the one who flitted about and managed those superficial interactions with ease.

My thoughts circled back to Fiona. While this intimacy shimmered in the air between us, and there was an ease to being with her, it was like trying to wear an uncomfortable shirt, one where the shoulders were too tight and the fabric itched on your skin. I wasn't comfortable with intimacy. I assumed I would always live alone. Lord knows I had enough brothers and sisters to have a whole passel of nieces and nephews. I could be the uncle who spoiled them with gifts.

This woman who I shouldn't even be looking at held me in thrall. Even if she didn't directly answer to me at the restaurant, I knew I needed to tread this line very carefully.

Instead, all I could think about was when I would see her next and finding a way to get her into my office where I could bend her over and fuck her on my desk.

Chapter Ten

BLAKE

Five full days passed before I encountered Fiona closely at work again. We had a brief encounter when I let her know her brakes were fixed. She'd been too busy to chat long and had thanked me, but that was it.

Oh, she was around. I saw her, typically moving at lightning speed while she worked in the kitchen, chatting with David about menu specials and smiling politely when the line cooks bantered among themselves. Whether by coincidence or deliberately on her part, I didn't cross her path in a way where we could speak privately for too long for my preference.

By the time that moment arrived, the anticipation of it and this deep craving inside to see her and speak to her burned like a hot coal.

I walked down the back hallway, where we had the brewing and winemaking rooms. The restaurant staff weren't often back here unless they needed something from one of the dry storage areas.

It was late, and, as usual, I was still working. I didn't mind working at all. I was back there checking the production schedule for the next run of a limited-edition beer that would go out for the fall. I heard the soft tread of shoes on the floor. Reflexively, I glanced out only to see the flick of a skirt disappearing as someone walked into a doorway.

Fiona always wore skirts that fell below her knees. She paired them with these cute cushioned tennis shoes.

I wouldn't even pretend I wasn't thinking about her. I absolutely wanted to see Fiona again, and I didn't care to consider otherwise.

I set down my notebook. I walked to the doorway of the brewing storage room and peered out into the hallway. No one else was nearby. I quickly crossed the hallway and slipped into the storage room. The door closed automatically, the soft whooshing sound following me when I stepped into the room. Fiona was looking at the shelves, leaning over as she peered into a row of spices.

"We need more of this," she said to herself. "I'll make a note."

I didn't attempt to hide my presence, but I also didn't make it known. I walked across the room until I was closer.

"Fiona."

She straightened quickly, dropping the large plastic container of spices she held. It fell to the floor with a little thump before it began rolling. Her blue eyes were wide and a flush rose on her cheeks as she looked at me.

Maybe I shouldn't have said what I did next. I couldn't take it back, though. "You came all over my fingers the last time I saw you."

Her mouth fell open in a pretty little "O" before she snapped it shut quickly. The flush on her cheeks deepened. "Blake!" she hissed.

My cock was already swelling with need for her. Sweet hell. This woman had a hold on me, and I sensed she had no idea.

"My apologies," I said quickly.

She laced her hands together just in front of her waist, one of her thumbs rubbing on a silver ring on her pinky.

"I'm curious," I began.

"About what" she whispered.

"Have you been avoiding me?" My question fell through the charged space between us.

Fiona's hands tightened. Her eyes dipped down before they lifted again. "Of course, I have." Her eyes shifted toward the door.

I decided to solve that little problem, turning and walking quickly over to turn the bolt. I was back in front of her in a matter of seconds. "There, now you don't have to worry about anyone walking in."

She took a quick breath, uncertainty chasing through her gaze. Suddenly, my need to provoke her, to make her remember just how good it was for us when I kissed her and she came apart dissipated.

Protectiveness rose swiftly inside. "You don't need to worry," I said, my tone low.

"That's easy for you to say," she said, twisting her lips as she rolled her eyes. "You and your family own Fireweed Industries. I know that David is my boss, but I kind of think of everyone in the family as my boss. If anyone found out, the way people would look at me is different from the way they would look at you."

She had a point, a very good point. I knew she was giving me an exit ramp for this highway of insanity and recklessness. Except

I didn't want it. I wanted her. I wanted to kiss her again, to unwrap her like a present, to lose myself in the fire that burned hotter and higher by simply being near her.

With that recklessness driving me, I stepped closer, lifting a hand and brushing a single lock of hair away from her forehead and smoothing it back. "I know."

Her teeth sank into the side of her lip, and I remembered how her lips felt underneath mine, plush and soft. My cock swelled, and I could feel the very beat of my heart in it.

She let out a frustrated sigh. "Blake."

"Fiona, I want you. I promise I will keep it quiet. I want you so much that I can't be sensible." She stared at me, and her lips parted slightly. "Tell me to walk away."

She shifted on her feet, and I knew, I just *knew*, she was wet.

"I don't want you to walk away," she whispered.

I didn't know what it was about this woman. I felt this craving for her that demolished logic and reason.

I stepped closer. "I'll stop whenever you say so."

I reached for her hands, lifting them together over her head. Her breasts jutted out.

I took another step closer, letting out a growl when I felt the warmth of her body against mine.

As I bent low, her scent reached me, a hint of sugar mingled with musk. I dropped hot kisses along the side of her neck, savoring the way she shivered in my arms and the little whimper that came from her throat.

"Blake," she rasped, my name laced with a plea.

I lifted my head, and it felt as if lightning sizzled in the air around us when our eyes collided. My heartbeat echoed in a drumroll through my body.

"What is it?"

"I have to go back to the kitchen." Her tongue slid across her lips, and my arousal swelled.

"Okay," I finally said, even though my body was screaming for me not to step away from her. "I just need to know one thing."

"What?"

I released her hands, and her arms fell. She curled her palms around the edges of the shelf behind her hips. I slid my palm down her side, resisting the urge to cup her breast. My touch moved over the sweet curve of her hip and down her thigh until I reached the hem of her skirt. "Are you wet?"

She let out the tiniest gasp as she stared at me, lifting her chin slightly when I hooked my fingers on the edge of her skirt. I almost groaned at the feel of her bare skin, silky soft, and smooth. I slid my palm up her thigh. She shifted on her feet just enough that I could tease my fingers between her thighs. Her silk panties were wet.

It took all of my restraint not to go further, not to tease my fingers into her very core. She let out a little whimper of protest when I slid my hand back down her thigh and tucked her skirt into place before I stepped away. My mind was a jumble; my thoughts hazed with a fierce need for her. I sucked in a deep breath, trying to clear my thoughts. I shook my head, and my eyes landed on the bottle of spice she'd been holding in her hand when I came in.

I picked it up and returned to where she still waited by the shelf. "Here." I handed it to her. My fingers tingled with the burn of her touch when they brushed against her.

"Blake, this is crazy." She straightened, finally stepping away from the shelving.

That vulnerability flickered in her eyes again. I wanted to fold her into my arms and promise her everything would be okay because I would make it so.

"Maybe it is," I finally said. "But I want you, and I think you want me too."

Her eyes dipped down, and she spun the plastic bottle in her hands. She looked back up at me. She surprised me when she said, "I do."

"When do you close again?" Even though I didn't manage the kitchen and never had, I knew they rotated whoever closed.

Nobody came back into this area that late. Because I tended to be a night owl by nature, I liked working late. It was my most productive time.

On the heels of a deep breath, she lifted her chin. "Three nights from now."

"You decide. I'll be in my office."

With that, I clung to the thin thread of discipline keeping me in check, then turned and left.

Chapter Eleven

FIONA

I opened the door quietly when I got home that night. As soon as it closed behind me, I glanced over to see my mom on the couch with a bowl of popcorn in her lap and Lia sound asleep beside her. My mom was watching another home sales show, her favorite guilty pleasure. She smiled over at me.

I slipped out of my shoes and left my purse on the small table by the door before walking over to the couch. I sat down beside my daughter, smoothing my hand over her hair. "I'll put her to bed."

Lia was just shy of being too heavy for me to carry. I experienced a sweet twinge in my heart as I lifted her carefully. She curled against my shoulder, letting out a sleepy sigh.

Parenting a child was so hard and so much work. I imagined most parents experienced the guilt I did about being impatient for them to get older so they didn't feel like an extension of their own body all the time. But then, you also knew it slipped away so fast. I knew the day when I wouldn't be able to pick her up was coming. She would be too heavy, and I would miss that time.

Fortunately, our apartment was small. By the time I got her down the short hallway to her bedroom, my arms were already getting tired. Because my mom was the absolute best, Lia was already changed into her pajamas. I was confident she had brushed her teeth and washed her hands and face.

My mom had even folded back the covers, so I could lay her down easily and tuck them over her. Lia never even woke up. She mumbled something when I tucked her in, but she instantly found her favorite stuffed animal, curling her elbow around it and holding it to her side. I watched her for a moment before leaning over and dusting a kiss on her forehead. I tiptoed out of the room, making sure her nightlight was on. I left the door just barely open. That was how she liked it.

When I returned to the kitchen area, I

filled a glass of water, calling over to my mother, "Need anything?"

"I've got everything," she returned. When I glanced over my shoulder, she held up her own glass of water and tossed some popcorn into her mouth.

I plunked down on the couch beside her, reaching over for a handful of popcorn. I took a bite, smiling at the subtle salty, sweet flavor. "You made the kettle corn."

"Don't talk while you're chewing," she teased.

I shrugged before chasing the popcorn down with a swallow of water and setting my glass on the coffee table. "How was your day?" I asked.

My mother, because she was ever re-sourceful, had already created her own small cleaning business. She had become fast friends with the owners of Spill The Beans Café, and started cleaning for them on the weekends. They had already connected her with several other places. She insisted she loved cleaning because it was meditative. Also, she could do it and work around Lia's schedule.

I honestly didn't know what I would do without her. Daycare was wildly expensive. Not that I resented the cost of daycare.

Taking care of children was really important and worth good money. I just didn't have the money to pay for it. With my mom's help, I had been able to find decent-paying jobs and scramble by.

"My day was good," she said. "I did two deep cleans today, and I'm going to need some more assistance with homework on the days you're not working in the evening. This new math stuff is confusing." She rolled her eyes.

I burst out laughing. My mom and I took turns sharing the popcorn as she caught me up on the status of the current show. "The husband in this one is foolish."

"Really?"

"Absolutely. He's indecisive." She tsk-tsked. "How was your day?"

"Good," I said. I really liked my job. I loved cooking, and the work environment in the kitchen was great. David could be a little cranky, but once you learned that was just his way, it was fine. He set a good tone, and everyone worked well as a team.

My mind flashed to the maybe three minutes that had passed with Blake. My body was still buzzing from the electrifying force of that encounter. I knew, I absolutely *knew*, it was stupid to let anything happen between us.

Oh sure, he wasn't technically my supervisor. But he was a part of the Cannon family who owned a whole fucking corporation. I was so far below him on the social stratification scale that it was beyond ridiculous. If he knew anything about my past, he would be horrified.

Yet the way I felt with him was like nothing I'd ever experienced before. Even though I'd been young and stupid, I sure had some fun with Lia's father, Johnny. Before I got pregnant, before he went from a casual dealer of prescription stimulants in high school to a major player in the local market, before it felt like his life skidded out of control, Johnny had been good to me.

But that was nothing like the way I felt with Blake. I knew the forbidden aspect of it was clouding my judgment.

"I'm glad you like it there," my mother said, hopefully oblivious to my unsettled state.

"I do. I really do."

"I like this town too," she added. "People are really nice here. It's a good change for you and Lia."

"And you?" I prompted gently.

Her smile was warm as she nodded.

My heart squeezed slightly. Because it had been a good change for Lia. After Johnny died, it had been hard for all of us. For all of his faults, including the fact that his own actions had led to his death because he was reckless, he tried to be a good father. He'd been loving and playful and always made sure to help out financially, even after we broke up. He had respected my decision on that. He wanted us to stay free of his entanglements. When he died, Lia had been devastated.

"Do you think she's been doing better?"

My mom nodded, her eyes studying me for a moment. "Don't you?"

I took a quick breath before letting it out. "I do. I suppose the change of scenery has helped."

Chapter Twelve

FIONA

One morning a few days later, I didn't have to be in to work until ten o'clock, so I decided to walk down for coffee after I walked Lia to school. It was late summer with a salty breeze gusting off the ocean. I smiled as I walked down the sidewalk, savoring the crisp air. Fireweed Harbor was a cute little town with colorful storefronts. The view was really something. The town sat against the feet of the mountains with a glacier nearby, and the harbor was visible from almost anywhere in the downtown area.

I reached Spill The Beans Café, smiling at the sign with the letters in shimmery pink and coffee beans spilled underneath them. As usual, there was a line when I walked in. I glanced around. It was always bright and cheerful here and smelled yummy with the scents of coffee and baked goods drifting through the air. The café had a view of Main Street with the harbor just beyond that. There were tables scattered about the space with a counter at the back and a large chalkboard mounted behind it. The chalkboard had some serious flair with everything written in cheerful font and flowers decorating the corners.

When I finally reached the counter, Haven smiled over at me. "Good morning."

"Hey! I didn't know you were still working here," I replied with a smile.

Haven Rivers was one of the first people I got to know when I moved to Fireweed Harbor. She often waited on me when I stopped by here to get coffee. I had quickly learned that this café was the heartbeat of the town. Gossip, the latest weather updates, and more flowed as generously as the coffee.

She waggled her brows. "I'll fill you in. Your usual?"

"Yes, please. Add an extra shot."

I liked a strong Americano. I'd tossed and turned last night as I played those brief moments with Blake on a loop in my thoughts. I needed the extra caffeine.

"You got it."

"And I'll take one of the toasted cranberry orange muffins," I added.

Haven popped the muffin in the oven and began prepping my coffee. "I'm just filling in," she explained. "I have officially become full-time at the marketing department at Fireweed Industries, but I told Hazel and Phyllis that whenever they needed a little extra help to call me. It isn't just for them. I actually love being here. I enjoy making coffee. I can't have any right now, though." She smoothed her hand over the curve of her belly. She'd told me before she was pregnant.

"And catching up on all of the local gossip," a voice said from over my shoulder.

I glanced back to see Rhys Cannon, Haven's boyfriend and the CEO of Fireweed Industries. He was Blake's older brother. I'd met him for the first time when I interviewed for the chef position. Although David was the one hiring me, he'd wanted feedback on my sample dishes.

Rhys was just as handsome as Blake. His dark-blond hair was a shade lighter than Blake's, and they shared similar silvery-gray eyes. Yet I felt absolutely no spark when I looked at Rhys, just an objective appreciation of his good looks.

Haven cast him a smile, her cheeks flushing slightly. "Of course. I have to stay up to speed," she teased.

Rhys glanced at me, dipping his chin. "Hello, Fiona. How are things in the kitchen at Fireweed Winery?"

"Good, I think."

Haven handed me my coffee, and I passed over some cash. "Thank you and keep the change."

"Things in the winery restaurant are better than good," Haven said. "Seeing as I *do* keep up on all the gossip here." She winked. "Everyone loves the updated menu, even David."

"Agreed," Rhys offered. "I ran into him the other day, and he's happy with you. We were all a little worried when David told us he wanted to phase out of his chef duties. He's particular, so we weren't sure how someone new would fit in, especially with him managing."

I smiled, taking a swallow of my coffee before replying, "He is. I was a little worried, but he seems pleased. He's been more relaxed than I expected about letting me make changes on the menu."

Rhys chuckled. "Once you get to know David, he's a soft touch, but he can come off as a little bossy at first. I'm glad it's working out. Now you're stuck here. He's been with us for over twenty years. We expect the same from you."

My eyes widened as he grinned. Haven chimed in, "He's teasing."

I shrugged. "I'm very happy there. Plus, I like Fireweed Harbor, and I have a daughter, so stability is what I'm after."

Rhys studied me for a moment before nodding. "Well, you can certainly find that here."

"Plus, our school system is really good," Haven offered.

"That's what I hear. Definitely a bonus."

Just then, the oven chimed, and Haven turned to get my muffin out.

"Here you go." She handed me the small paper bag.

"Good to see you both," I said as I waved and turned to walk out.

I was walking along the sidewalk, sipping my coffee when I decided to take a detour down to the harbor. I had enough time before I needed to get to the winery. I enjoyed sitting on the benches that looked out over the harbor.

Settling down in a sunny area, I sipped my coffee and broke off pieces of my muffin as I watched the activity in the harbor. The view was stunning with the sun coming up over the mountains behind the town and casting sparks on the surface of the water. Mist was rising above the small islands visible out beyond the harbor.

I hoped someday I could take a boat out and see the islands. An eagle called, the sound piercing and closer than expected. Glancing over, I saw one of the large birds lifting off a piling near the top of the docks. I watched the eagle as it soared high, looking down. In a flash, it dove, its talons stretching wide as it scooped up a fish in the water. I let out a startled breath.

Just then, I heard footsteps behind me and glanced over my shoulder to see Blake approaching. He smiled at me, nudging his chin toward the eagle as it rose up with the fish firmly clasped in its grip. "They're better at fishing than most humans," he commented.

He stopped beside me, and we watched together as the eagle flew beyond the edge of the harbor to land on a small stretch of beach nearby with rocks and gray sand. "I guess he's having breakfast there," I offered.

Blake glanced my way again, and it felt as

if a flame flickered in the air between us. "Mind if I join you?"

Butterflies took flight, twirling inside my belly and sending sparks scattering through me.

"Of course not." I scooted over a little bit, setting the small bag down beside my hips, as if that flimsy paper bag could create any kind of barrier to contain my body's reaction to him.

His eyes landed on the paper coffee cup held in my hand, emblazoned with the distinctive logo for Spill The Beans Café. "I see you know where to get the best coffee in town."

"Don't we make the best coffee at Fireweed Winery?" I teased.

Blake flashed a quick grin. My belly reacted with a dizzying flip.

"I think our restaurant makes excellent coffee for a restaurant. But the café has the best coffee in town."

I felt my cheeks heat as I looked at him. "They do. We don't specialize in coffee."

He nodded and looked out toward the harbor. "Do you come down here often?"

I dragged my gaze away from him, watching a boat pull out of its slip, its motor humming. Fishing boats were readying to go out, and people walked back and forth on the docks, talking to each other and doing all kinds of things.

"I do." I glanced over at him. "The view is beautiful, of course. But I also like watching the people on the docks. I have no idea what they're doing, but it's kind of relaxing to watch."

His lips kicked up at one corner, yet again sending my belly into a flip. "It is. I love coming down here. Have you been out on the water yet?" He gestured beyond the harbor toward what I knew to be the famed Inside Passage.

I finished the last bite of my muffin. "Just the ferry trip here, which was beautiful. I haven't had a chance to do more. The tourist boats are expensive."

"They are. It's cheaper come fall. I could take you out. Do you think Lia and your mom would like to go?"

It warmed my heart that he immediately thought of Lia and my mother. I wouldn't want to do something like that without them. "I'd love that," I replied before I could think better of it.

"You just let me know when, and I'll take you out."

We sat there, our gazes locked. Entangled

within my body's fierce response to Blake was this unfamiliar sense of comfort. It was unsettling to be attracted to him, and my rational brain knew it was a mistake to let anything happen. That knowledge tossed me into a place of uncertainty. I didn't know where this could carry me, carry us, yet I somehow felt like I knew him, like I understood him. In return, I felt as if he understood me in a way no one else did. As if I could be completely myself with him.

As long as he didn't realize what an idiot I'd been when I was younger. Blake Cannon likely had no idea just how far apart we were on the scale of social stratification. I was the girl who came from a poor family. There was a lot of love, but my parents had scraped by. I'd been reckless in high school and fallen for a guy who loved me, but who was also a criminal. It had been so very stupid, just like getting pregnant when I was too young and too ashamed to tell anyone until it was too late to do anything.

Despite the epic disaster of my reckless youth, the absolute best thing that came out of it was my daughter. My love for Lia was so big I couldn't even contain it in my heart. I wouldn't change that for anything. I would take all of the mess with it.

I felt hot all over, heat blooming from the center of me and radiating outward. My phone vibrated, chirping the alarm that reminded me I needed to get to work. I was so caught up in staring into Blake's eyes that I jumped, letting out a startled squeak at the sound.

His low chuckle sent a shiver chasing down my spine. "Does your phone usually scare you?"

I fumbled for it in my purse. "Sometimes." I glanced back up at him. "I have to go."

He stood with me. "I'm sure I'll see you around work at some point today."

Only then did it occur to me that tonight was my late night. *The* night. If I wanted it.

I shouldn't have felt this way, but I was reluctant to leave him. The pull to him was almost magnetic. I had to force my feet to turn and walk away as I waved.

FIONA

Hours later, I was busy at work. I often felt like I was spinning plates when I was in the kitchen, dashing from one task to the next. Everything was a balancing act. I loved the pace of it, though. I could fall into a rhythm with each task flowing into the next.

I finished up a run of orders, glancing up to see I was all caught up. I looked over toward Tommy, the closest line cook. "Be right back. I'm going to zip out for a bathroom break."

He simply nodded, flipping a burger, the sizzle and steam rising above the stove. I hurried out of the kitchen and down the hallway to the break room. Moments later, I was walking out of the bathroom, looking down as I adjusted the tie on my apron, and collided with someone.

I knew it was Blake even before I looked up. His scent was now familiar to me, woodsy with a hint of salt. I lifted my eyes to find him looking down at me.

I jumped back with a little squeak. We were shielded by the door as he held it open with his hand near the top of it. As we stared at each other, I could hear the rush of blood in my ears with every echoing beat of my heart. I licked my lips and swallowed.

Blake's eyes darkened.

Chapter Fourteen

BLAKE

"I have to get to the kitchen," Fiona said, her voice breathy.

The urge to nudge her back into the bathroom and kiss her senseless was so powerful that I almost acted on it. I managed not to, but just barely. I shackled the raw need roaring through me like a river in spring.

"Of course." I stepped back, and she brushed past me, the subtle touch of her elbow on my side like a sizzle of fire, burning through the fabric of my shirt and singeing my skin. I was losing my mind over this woman.

Tonight was *the* night. Maybe.

I was relieved to be busy at work. Typically, I preferred to be busy. Yet it was more than that now. Ever since Fiona had appeared in my orbit, I craved the distraction. We were ramping up planning and production for our special edition season. Autumn into winter was when we focused on testing out new products. For the most part, they all stayed seasonal and for a limited time, but the holiday season gave us the opportunity to see how things held up with sales. If something was wildly popular, we would consider making it a regular product. Autumn was a natural time to follow trends. Alaska had plentiful berries to incorporate into beers, wines, and meads.

I had video conferences with several of our distributors and checked in with our brewer. I mulled over potential legal action over a brewery in Seattle mimicking all of our products. I wasn't one to get too tied up over that. Everybody followed the themes and trends, but we had a few trademarked items in our recipes. One of our distributors that handled storage in the Seattle area had caught wind of the issue.

I tapped the speaker button on my phone, quickly calling Quinn Blackthorn. Her family had handled the legal stuff for Fireweed Industries for decades. She even had an office over in the main offices for the corporation.

"Hey, Blake," Quinn answered.

"Do you have my number memorized?" I teased lightly.

"No, but I have you in my contacts," Quinn replied dryly.

"Ah, well that makes sense."

I heard a voice in the background. "Is that my brother?"

Kenan and Quinn had been close friends for years. It was totally platonic, according to both of them, although I personally thought they would make a good couple. The one time I had suggested it to Kenan, he'd looked so horrified I believed there was no spark there.

I heard the smile in Quinn's voice when she replied, "That would be Kenan. He just dropped a coffee off for me from Spill the Beans Café. I'm up to my eyeballs in looking over contracts, so I needed the good stuff."

"Mind asking him if he can swing back by there and bring one over to me?"

"Let me put you on speaker."

"Hey, little brother," I called.

"Hey, Blake." Kenan chuckled. "Do you need legal advice today?"

"Of course, I do. I'd call Quinn just to

check in, but it's actually a business call today."

"Should I step out?" Kenan asked.

"It's not personal. It's business."

"Even if it was personal, wouldn't you want my feedback?" he teased.

Quinn laughed. "Blake, what's going on?" Her tone shifted to all business.

I quickly explained the situation, ending with, "So our guy down there thinks they're copying our Beer & Berries Line."

"Ah, we need to nip that in the bud," Kenan said as soon as I finished explaining.

"It should be fairly straightforward," Quinn interjected. "I'll send a letter, and that should take care of it. Leave it to me. If I need to touch base with you about it again, I'll call over."

"And this is exactly why you're awesome," I replied.

"It's my job. Literally," Quinn returned.

"Hey, Kenan," I said.

"Yeah?"

"Mind getting me a coffee?"

"You going to tip me?" he teased.

"Did Quinn?"

My brother's laughter rumbled through the line. "No, she did not. If you say please. I was actually going to go from here to the winery. So swinging by Spill the Beans is on my way."

"Please," I said with a flourish.

"You got it. I'll see you in a few."

I thanked Quinn and ended that call. After that, I started to look at my email, but my cell phone vibrated on my desk again. I glanced down, surprised to see my brother Wyatt's name flash on the screen.

Wyatt, Griffin, and McKenna were the youngest of us. Until Jake died, it had felt like there were three groups of us. Jake, Rhys, and me as the three oldest. Then Adam and Kenan who were just shy of two years younger than me. Then Griffin and Wyatt were another two years behind them with McKenna the youngest by another year.

As hotshot firefighters, Griffin and Wyatt happened to work up in Fairbanks on a crew with Deacon, Rhys's best friend from high school. Wyatt and Griffin were close, but of the whole family, Wyatt kept himself at a distance. I could only hope someday I would find out why.

I tapped my phone screen to answer. "Hey, Wyatt. Good to hear from you. What's up?"

"Hey, man. Just doing my occasional check-in. You know how I like to do that."

Wyatt and I shared the tendency to keep things light. "Oh, your monthly check-in," I said dryly. "Things are pretty good here, if you're wondering. Anytime you decide to take a break from fighting fires, I've got a job for you at the winery. My main brewing guy and his wife are having a baby. He let me know he might be moving to Juneau. If that happens, I'll be looking for a new brewer."

"I'll keep it in mind," Wyatt said without offering anything further.

We chatted briefly, discussing entirely superficial issues. Then he said something that perked my ears up. "Oh, you remember Monica?"

"My girlfriend from high school?"

"Yeah, the only girlfriend I knew you to have. I mean, you date, but you and Monica were whatever serious was in high school."

I circled my hand in the air even though he couldn't see. "Of course, I remember Monica. Nice enough girl until she screwed around on me."

"Oh yeah, she broke your heart," Wyatt said.

My laugh was dry. My feelings about Monica had been youthful. In hindsight, I thought the only thing she did was contribute to the cynicism that I already carried inside about whether or not romance was worth it.

Family was worth it, but my memories of my father were so vague that I couldn't even say for sure if he and my mom had a great marriage. I only recalled that he had been a good father and I loved him. Then he was gone, and our grandfather started making our lives hell.

"What about Monica?" I prompted.

"I ran into her at the grocery store. I guess she and her husband moved up here. Looks like she's looking to get out of her marriage. They've got three kids, and she hit on me. I told her to take a hike." Wyatt sounded legitimately annoyed.

I rolled my eyes. "I guess she hasn't changed her ways. So why are you telling me this?"

I honestly hadn't contemplated Monica since maybe high school when it all went down. Her family moved away after high school, so she wasn't on my radar.

"Because she told me to tell you hey and said she hopes you're doing well."

"I guess if you see her again, you can give her my regards. You coming down for a visit anytime soon?"

"Not sure. We're still dealing with fires.

I'll make sure I'm there for Thanksgiving and Christmas if not sooner."

"Mom would love that."

"I'll be there." There was a sound in the background. "Gotta roll," Wyatt said.

We ended the call, and I briefly thought about Monica. We'd started dating in high school. It lasted for a whole year. I snorted to myself, realizing Wyatt was right. It was my longest relationship. My cynicism had already been deeply seated by that point. I'd seen the ugly way my grandfather had treated my grandmother and my mother's lingering grief after losing our father. I'd been fending for myself, maybe serious about Monica. She'd gotten caught making out with another guy under the bleachers during lunch at school one day, and that had been that. Monica had attempted to reach out to me once after we broke up. She had come to Fireweed Harbor for a visit while she was in college. By then, I sensed she'd developed a level of awareness about my family's situation that she didn't have before. She'd tried to persuade me to give her a chance, but I hadn't been interested, not even a little.

By the time I was in college, I had discovered the benefits of casual relationships and enjoyed them thoroughly. At thirty-one years old now, I was busy with a rewarding career in my family's business. I didn't have much time to even consider relationships. These days, I had the occasional weekend fling in Juneau. I tried not to date in Fireweed Harbor, if only because the small town meant too many potential complications.

I'd made that mistake once, only once, and still had to deal with those threads. A friendly acquaintance who worked at the bank had flirted with me over the years. It had been light and teasing and nothing more. I finally had a night with her. She was the one who'd laid out the ground rules, telling me she didn't like things to get serious and she wanted to make sure I understood that. Come to find out, she later told me she only said that because she thought I wouldn't even consider it otherwise. Ellen had come crying to me in my office a mere two weeks after our one night together, telling me she felt like I didn't see the *real* her and all that we could have.

That was three years ago. Whenever I saw her at the bank now, she still gave me the side-eye even though she was married with a kid.

Monica taught me a valuable lesson, and Ellen a different one. This train of thought led me straight to Fiona. She had so many warning signs around her that should've sent me running. I didn't even want to contemplate why I shouldn't act on my feelings. I simply wanted her.

Chapter Fifteen

BLAKE

It was getting late, but the kitchen was still busy. I knew things would be winding down soon. I also knew the general routine even though David fully managed the restaurant. That had been the arrangement when I took over at the brewery and winery. I honestly didn't want to run a restaurant. The only reason I crossed paths with the staff there so often was because it was in the same location as our production. I also enjoyed running the events for the brewery and winery.

I told myself I was just doing my usual loop through the place when I circled the building, peering into the brewing area, which was quiet. Our main brewer, George, had a pencil tucked behind his ear and was staring at a notebook when I paused in the doorway.

"What are you doing here so late?" I asked.

He glanced over, flashing a quick smile. "I'm about to head out. I was just checking my notes for the upcoming schedule. You know I like to write everything down by hand."

"I do. Seeing as I do the same, I understand."

I waved as I continued, passing by the prep area where the kitchen staff got things ready for the following morning. Just as I expected, Fiona was there. She didn't even notice me walking by because she was jotting something down on a notepad.

I forced myself to keep moving. I stopped in to chat with David, telling myself that I was just doing what I would normally do. Maybe I was.

A few minutes later, I passed back by the kitchen prep room and heard a muffled sob.

I looked through the doorway. Fiona stood with her back to the door, holding her cell phone to her ear, her hand clenching it tightly. After another moment, she lowered the phone. I saw her shoulders shake. Protectiveness rose swiftly inside. It was all I could do not to cross the room and pull her into my arms. I didn't even know what was wrong.

With Fiona, none of my reactions made sense.

FIONA

I heard footsteps stop in the hallway and quickly slipped my phone into the pocket of my apron, pulling my sleeve down over the heel of my hand and dabbing at the tears damp on my cheeks. Blessedly, the footsteps resumed.

Glancing over my shoulder, I walked toward the doorway and peered out. There was no one visible now. I walked back to where I'd been working, staring blindly at the small notebook where I was crossing off everything the brunch crew would need in the morning.

I was already at the bottom of my list. I checked on the last item and crossed it off. I pulled my phone out, once again lifting it to my ear after tapping to play the voicemail.

This is a message for Fiona Thompson. This is Gerald, I used to work with Johnny. I don't know who you talked to, but you need to stay quiet.

My heartbeat raced unsteadily, and I felt a little sick. I didn't know Gerald. But I didn't know a lot of things about Johnny's life. I most definitely didn't know what the hell this guy was talking about.

When Johnny died, he and I had been broken up for two years. He helped out with bills because he was decent like that, but that was it. He knew I wanted nothing to do with the mess he'd gotten himself into.

It felt as if all of my bad decisions had followed me to Alaska. I hadn't been running from anything when I came here. Yet I had genuinely wanted a fresh start, a change of scenery in a place where I felt like I could make a life that wasn't tainted by the mistakes I'd made when I was younger.

I heard footsteps again and reflexively glanced over. Blake was walking by. He paused, his sharp gaze landing on me instantly. "You okay?"

I wanted to run over and fling myself into his arms. Because I knew Blake was strong, and maybe he could make me forget everything.

As he stood there, studying me for no

more than a few seconds, it felt as if he could see right through me, into the fear flooding inside my chest. I managed to take a deep breath, telling myself to stay calm, and that it was nothing.

I nodded, lifting my chin and straightening my shoulders as if I could will my fear away.

"Yeah," I finally replied.

His eyes held mine through several echoing beats of my heart before he dipped his chin in acknowledgment. I sensed he didn't believe me. But we were winding down in the kitchen after the rush of dinner. Although the crush of orders had ended, this part of the night was just as busy for me.

I kept telling myself not to think about the fact that tonight was *that* night. The night when Blake said he would be waiting for me in his office if I wanted to find him. I must've replayed our two wild kisses, and then some, in my thoughts hundreds of times. I kept telling myself it wasn't smart. It was downright reckless to walk to his office tonight after everybody left.

Yet nothing in me was feeling sensible. My fierce need for him, pure and elemental, was riding roughshod over my ability to be sensible.

He's not technically your boss. David is.

Hahahaha! My cynical mind taunted me.

As if the universe was trying to play a joke on me, that evening I stopped by David's office to check with him about some menu specials.

Blake's mother, Claire Cannon, happened to walk by, peering into the office and smiling at us. "I just wanted to say I loved the lemon halibut dish tonight." She lifted her fingertips to her mouth, blowing a chef's kiss.

David chuckled, and I thanked her. After she left, I asked, "Is there any other feedback from the family about the changes we've made to the menu?"

"They all love it, but you don't answer to them. Keep that in mind." When I wrinkled my nose and eyed him uncertainly, David added, "I appreciate that you care what they think, and I won't pretend it doesn't matter at all, but it can get overwhelming. The Cannons are a big family with a lot of opinions. Plus, McKenna is allergic to shellfish."

That wasn't the first time David reminded me he ran the restaurant. So you see, David was on my side. He had no idea I was using his role as a reason to tell myself I didn't answer to Blake.

As these thoughts bounced through my

mind, every time I thought about my phone, it felt like a hot coal in my pocket. Tucked away in my purse, I didn't even want to look at it after that message earlier tonight. I told myself I didn't need to check my phone. My mom knew to call the restaurant if she needed me. She also knew I was working late. This was my extra-late night when I didn't even get home until after midnight.

Time and again, I sensed Blake's presence—when I saw him chatting with one of the guys who worked in the brewery as he was leaving and a while later when I heard David tease him for working too late as David left. It wasn't unusual for Blake to work late. As far as I could tell, he was a workaholic.

I had just about talked myself out of going to Blake's office when I went into the break room to prepare to leave. The muted hum of the voices from the bar barely reached me. Once the restaurant stopped serving and customers filtered out, almost no one came back here until the bar closed at two o'clock. Two bartenders worked out front with a bar back helping them.

They would all stay out front since the bar area was separate from the restaurant. With the beer and liquor storage in a room directly behind the bar, they didn't even walk down this hallway in the evenings.

I knew it was probably just Blake and me back here. That awareness alone sent shivers down my spine and goosebumps prickling over the surface of my skin. It was insane to even think about him.

I went to my locker, the sound loud as I opened the metal door. I tossed my chef's jacket into the laundry basket for the staff in the corner. When I saw my reflection in the small mirror on the inside of my locker, I hurried into the bathroom, splashing water on my face and washing my hands.

Although I'd had a long afternoon and evening, I didn't feel tired. Between that damned phone message and thinking about Blake, my entire nervous system was buzzing. When I walked back to my locker, I knew I had to check my phone, just in case.

My thumb had a mind of its own, sliding across the screen and checking my messages quickly. I didn't play the message again, but the transcription was there. Instantly, my mind started spinning, and that old anxiety and tangle of fear rose inside. It was from my days when Johnny was alive, and I had learned just how much trouble he was in.

Before I could think better of it, I stuffed

my phone in my purse and snatched it up, along with my jacket. Instead of my feet turning toward the staff entrance directly off the break room, I slipped out into the hallway, glancing furtively in both directions.

My footsteps were light and swift down the hallway before I pushed through the swinging doors that delineated the brewery from the restaurant area. This was the production zone and where Blake's office was. I couldn't even hear the muted sounds of the bar from here.

The hallway was mostly dark except for where light spilled out of one office. I could hear the rush of blood in my ears with every beat of my heart.

I stopped maybe ten feet away from the doorway into Blake's office. I tried to take a breath, but my lungs weren't cooperating. The mere anticipation of walking through that doorway and what it might mean had need sinking its claws into me. My breath was shallow with my heartbeat galloping like a wild pony.

Before I took another step, Blake appeared in the doorway. His eyes met mine, and I was instantly caught in his gaze. I couldn't look away, and it felt as if a line connected us, snapping, crackling, and sending sparks shimmering into the air between us.

He waited with one hand resting on the inside of the doorjamb. I sensed he paused to make sure this was my choice. My belly shimmied, sending a scatter of tingling sparks through me. I took one step and then another.

Inside of a blazing-hot second, I stood in front of him. I could feel the heat of him, his strength emanating. The craving to lose myself in his strength and our desire, my awareness of the sense of protection he carried, all rose swiftly inside me again.

His hand fell from where it had been resting, and he caught one of mine in his as he stepped back. "Come here," he said, his voice low and gruff.

Seconds later, we were inside his office, and he closed the door behind us, the sound of it clicking shut was loud in the quiet space. I had only been in here once before. My eyes arced about the space. His desk faced the doorway, with his chair behind it against the back wall. I knew a window to the side offered a view of trees.

I suddenly worried about that window in the bright light. As if he could read my mind, Blake dropped my hand and turned. Taking three quick strides to the window, he tugged the shade down over it.

I remained standing in front of the closed door, frozen in place. My body was alive and thrumming with a cacophony of sensations. Arousal was slick between my thighs, need prickled over my skin, and heat radiated through me.

Blake returned to stand in front of me, reaching beyond my shoulder and flicking a light switch off. That left a lamp on the corner of his desk the only light. It felt as if we were all alone in the whole wide world.

"Are you okay?" His tone was careful, and I knew he was asking about that moment earlier when he had walked in and caught me at the tail end of crying.

I was, and I wasn't, but it was nothing I could share with him. Yet the fact he cared widened the fissure opening in my heart. The feelings he elicited were confusing. I wanted to chalk it up to lust, to the tricky way the universe created chemistry between some people. Sometimes it was foolish, and sometimes it made no sense.

For so many reasons, I shouldn't want Blake Cannon. I definitely shouldn't act on my desire for him. Yet something else shimmered between us, something deeper, a connection and a sense of knowing.

"I'm okay," I whispered.

He took a step closer and then another, and my back bumped into the door. "I want you, Fiona." He lifted a hand, his fingertips landing along the edge of my jaw. His feather-light touch was like a blaze of fire on my skin as he stroked across the surface.

I could hardly breathe. My belly felt tingly, almost ticklish. My need for him was a sweet, sharp pleasure that set my nerve endings alight. "I want you too," I rasped.

A second later, he dipped his head, dropping a kiss on one corner of my mouth and then the other. I arched into him, letting out a needy little sigh and biting my lip when he pressed hot, open-mouthed kisses on the side of my neck.

I shifted on my feet. Oh. My. God. I had never known desire like this before. Giving in to it sent oxygen rushing into the fire, fanning the flames wildly. All I wanted was to give myself over to it, to the rush of need and passion underlaid with an intense emotion. At this moment, I couldn't grasp the depth and power of the emotion. It was a first draft, the edges rough, and the full story not formed. Yet the power of it shimmered from the first word.

"Blake," I rasped, his name a plea.

"Yes, Fi?" He lifted his head, his eyes studying mine as I stood there, relieved to have a door behind me.

My knees were liquid, and I could feel the heartbeat of my desire echoing through every cell. "I need you."

My honesty shocked me. But I couldn't hide from him, and I didn't want to. Maybe later I would regret it. In fact, I was certain I would. But right now, caught in the very flame of this moment, I couldn't. My need was raw, elemental, the growl of a hungry animal in the snarl of a fight.

"I know." His eyes were dark as he held my gaze.

A blazing second passed before his mouth was on mine, and he pressed against me. I felt the hard length of his arousal against my low belly. Our kiss exploded—lips, teeth, and tongues tangling, fighting to get enough, nearly devouring each other.

By the time we broke apart, I gasped for air while he tugged at the buttons on my blouse, murmuring something before swearing, "Fuck me."

I felt cool air strike my skin as my blouse fell open. My nipples were already tight and achy. He wasted no time, undoing the clasp to my bra and letting out a growl before his mouth closed over a nipple. The sharp pleasure arrowed down to my throbbing pussy. I clenched, pressing my thighs together, trying to contain my need.

Blake lifted his head, reaching his hand down and yanking my skirt up. His eyes were locked on mine as he reached between my thighs, his palm cupping my mound. I felt the press of his fingers against the wet silk. I bit my lip, whimpering when he shoved my panties out of the way and delved into my swollen, slippery-wet folds.

"Oh, sweetheart," he whispered.

All I could do was pant in reply. He stepped back abruptly, and I cried out, bereft at the absence of his touch. We stared at each other. I nearly came on the spot when he reached down and dragged his palm over his cock, still buttoned up behind his jeans.

"I need to be inside you when you come," he said flatly.

I pushed away from the door on unsteady legs and stopped in front of him. "Please," I whispered, unashamed and so needy, so *very* needy.

He spun me around. Seconds later, I

stood in front of his desk, bending over as he shoved my skirt up. I felt his touch curving over my bottom before he yanked my panties down. I stepped out of them, kicking them free.

He pushed my open blouse up my back, dropping kisses on my skin. It felt like hot drops of lava, each kiss sending heat spiraling higher and higher, hotter and hotter inside.

I heard him murmur something, followed by the distinct sound of a condom wrapper opening. I glanced over my shoulder to see him swiftly rolling a condom on. When he caught my eyes, he straightened, lifting me, turning me, and sliding my hips on his desk.

"I need to see you," he rasped.

My skirt stretched tight around my thighs. As he pushed my knees apart, it rode up farther. I watched as his eyes dropped down. I should have felt some sense of reserve, but there was none.

His gaze lifted to mine as he dipped his fingers between my thighs and leaned down, bringing his mouth to my sex.

I was so close to release, my clit a swollen, needy bud. He licked deeply, his fingers delving inside just before he sucked lightly on my clit. I cried out sharply, my hips bucking against his mouth as my orgasm slammed into me.

Before I could even recover, he straightened, positioning his cock at my entrance and sliding in while I was still shuddering from my climax. He brought his mouth to mine, and I tasted the tang of my arousal as he kissed me.

He filled me completely and held still before lifting his mouth from mine. "Just one more. For me."

Chapter Seventeen

BLAKE

Fiona stared at me—her eyes dark, her lips kiss swollen, and her pussy clenching around my cock. Her tongue slid across her bottom lip when she nodded. "Okay," she whispered.

I was barely in control, clinging to the thinnest thread. I held still, savoring the feel of her tight and slick channel around me. After a beat, I drew back slowly, watching her as I sank inside and filled her again. I reached for her hips, pulling her closer to the edge of the desk. She curled her legs around my hips as I began to rock into her, fucking her slow and deep.

I had no idea how long it lasted. At this moment, I was utterly in thrall to this woman. Need sizzled through me with every thrust. Her little gasps and moans and whimpers drove me mad. My balls tightened, and I knew I was close.

I brought one hand between us to lightly circle my fingers over her plump clit. She cried out, going taut and shuddering as she came again.

I finally let go, my release drawing tight before snapping loose sharply when I thrust one final time. She curled into me, tucking her head in the curve of my neck as I slid one arm around her and held her close.

As I stood there holding Fiona, my pulse began to slow in the aftermath of my crashing release. I'd known I wanted Fiona. My desire for her was fierce, burning hotter and hotter as the days had passed since our first kiss.

Yet that awareness left me unprepared for the intimacy I felt with her. There was a closeness, a comfort I'd never experienced before. I'd always enjoyed sex, but it genuinely felt casual with my emotions at a distance.

As I felt the soft give of her skin where my hand still rested on her hip and the beat of her heart against my chest, I wanted to lift her into my arms and take her home with me. Not because I wanted more sex—although that was probably a foregone conclusion—but because I wanted to fall asleep with her beside me.

She lifted her head, tipping it back. Her gaze was almost level with mine as she sat on my desk. We stared at each other, and she looked as stunned as I felt. Her swallowing was audible as her eyes searched mine, uncertainty swirling there.

She took a quick breath, and I felt the gust of it on my skin when she released it. "Well," she finally said.

My lips tugged into a slight smile. "I should go," she added.

"Of course."

We disentangled ourselves, and moments later, Fiona looked tidy and put together. The only giveaway to the intensity of our encounter was the slight pink tinge on her cheeks.

I walked to my office door, reaching for the handle when her voice stopped me. "I don't think you should walk out with me."

I turned back. "Okay," I said reluctantly. I wanted every second I could have with her, even just walking by her side in the hallway.

Her hand curled more tightly around the strap of her purse where it hung over her shoulder. "I know David's my boss, but your family owns this place. It would be —" She bit her lip, letting out a frustrated sigh. "Not great if people knew what just happened."

I knew everything she said was logical. Of course, it was. But I didn't want this to be the end of the line for us. "What if I want to see you again?"

Her gaze held mine, and I could practically see the wheels turning in her brain. "You see me almost every day I'm working," she pointed out, neatly attempting to side-step my question.

"You know that's not what I mean, Fiona."

The tinge on her cheeks deepened. "I know," she said, her tone almost resigned.

I turned to face her more fully, taking a few steps until I stood right in front of her. Lifting a hand, I smoothed back a stray lock of hair that had fallen from her tidy bun. "What if I promised to keep it quiet? No one has to know."

She sucked in a breath as she stared at me, shifting on her feet. "Blake —"

Leaning down, I pressed a hot, open-mouthed kiss on the side of her neck, gratified when she arched into me. When I lifted my head, I asked, "Do you really want this to be it?"

"No," she whispered.

"Tell me your number." Stepping back, I slid my phone out of my pocket.

She recited her number, and I quickly tapped it into my phone before sending her a text.

"That's mine."

Chapter Eighteen

FIONA

Blake: *Your car is ready.*

I stared down at Blake's text. It was just a text. And still, butterflies spun in my belly and heat rolled through me. I smiled at those four words.

Before I had a chance to reply, his next text came in.

Blake: *I'm going to drop it off in the parking lot at your apartment.*

My lips twisted with a sigh. I was super worried about every interaction with Blake. Even though I knew I wasn't the only person in this place he did favors for. Not by a long shot. Just the other day, I overheard him and David talking about arranging the plowing for David's house for next winter. Apparently, Blake liked to plow snow.

Me: *Ok. I really appreciate your help. If you need a favor in return, just let me know.*

I slipped my phone into my purse and hurried from the break area out into the kitchen. It was the start of my shift for one of our busiest nights of the week.

The kitchen was a whirlwind of activity that evening, and I thrived on it. It helped that I absolutely loved cooking, but I craved anything to keep me distracted. Between the tornado of emotions spinning inside me around Blake, what had happened the other night, and the way that message from the same evening had burrowed into my worries, I needed something to keep my mind occupied.

"Fiona!" Tommy called over.

I glanced up from where I drizzled a sauce over some rice. "Yeah?"

"That halibut special you came up with this week?" He waggled his brows dramatically. "Fucking amazing. People love it. We've run out of halibut every single night."

"An eighty-six is your highest compliment," Phil chimed in.

I smiled, a sense of pride blooming in my chest. "It is. Thank you."

I didn't realize David had walked in until he stopped beside me. "You're doing great."

That was high praise from David, so I simply smiled. He cuffed me lightly on the shoulder as he passed by. By the time the evening was winding down, I was tired.

Tommy handled closing this evening, so I headed to the break room when the last order came through. After removing my hairnet and splashing water on my face, I slipped out of the bathroom. When I saw Blake over at the table in the corner, chatting with Phil, I schooled my expression to something bland.

I walked quickly over to the lockers, fetching my purse and coat. When I turned around, Phil was saying goodbye to Blake as he walked out the back door. Phil's eyes caught mine. "See you tomorrow," he called over.

"Thanks for everything," I called in return.

That left me alone in the break room with Blake. I was acutely aware that at any second someone else might pass through. Even though I was leaving for the night, servers remained in the restaurant, and Tommy was finishing up orders from the bar.

My eyes collided with Blake's. We had

maybe fifteen feet between us. The break room was spacious, but the room suddenly felt small. I willed the heat rising swiftly to cool down and prayed my cheeks didn't turn red. It was all pointless because I could feel the blush rising to the surface.

It felt as if cinders were falling all around us, scattering sparks through the air. I wanted to kiss Blake. I wanted to close the distance between us and let my hand fall to his chest so I could feel the beat of his heart, reminding me he was there, reminding me of that intense, elemental connection I felt with him. The force of it was so powerful I felt tugged in opposite directions—caught between the urge to let myself tumble into it, to be enthralled by it because it felt so very good, and the urge to scurry away, running as far and as fast as I could. Because I knew my heart was in danger.

"I dropped your car off like I said. It's in the parking lot behind your apartment." As if he could read my mind because he probably could—that was how crazy I felt around him—he added, "It's in parking spot two. That's your apartment, right?"

"How did you know?"

"Fireweed Property Management is part

of Fireweed Industries," he said matter-of-factly.

I let out a startled laugh. "Of course, it is."

Blake shrugged lightly. "I don't handle it, but I worked there in high school, helping with maintenance. So I'm familiar with most of the properties."

I swallowed and nodded, my hand tightening around the strap of my purse as we stood there. One of the servers came walking in. She glanced over. "Have a good night, Fiona. That halibut dish was delish," she said as she walked past. She tossed a quick smile in Blake's direction before slipping into the bathroom.

"I should go," I said.

The table in the corner was by the employee entrance. Blake reached for the door, holding it open for me as I walked over. The heat of his presence was like a blaze on my skin as I walked by.

"Good night, Fiona."

I couldn't even trust myself to speak, so I simply nodded. My eyes snagged his once more before I tore them away and walked out into the darkness. The evening air was cool on my cheeks. I took several deep breaths and began walking quickly through the parking area before turning toward the street.

I loved my job. I loved that I could walk home and feel safe.

I need to be careful and not screw this up.

I told myself I could resist Blake.

Lia was asleep when I got home, and my mom was dozing on the couch. I looked around our small apartment, my lips curling in a smile. Maybe it wasn't much, but I loved it. We had a cozy living room and kitchen and three whole bedrooms. They may be small bedrooms, but they were bedrooms. Until we moved here, I had shared my bedroom with my daughter. After I broke up with Johnny, I stayed with my parents. Then my dad passed, and it was just my mom, Lia, and me.

Lia barely woke up when I kissed her good night. I brushed my teeth, washed my face, and climbed into my own bed.

I had started to read when my phone vibrated on the small table beside my bed. I eyed it suspiciously. No one texted me this late, so curiosity got the best of me, and I reached for it. The moment my eyes saw Blake's name flash on the screen, my belly flipped. Heat flared on my cheeks, and I put the phone down quickly.

I tried to read my book, but my eyes kept sliding to my phone.

Laughing softly, I reached for it again after reading the same paragraph in my book three times.

Blake: *I want to see you again.*

Chapter Nineteen

BLAKE

I was at home, sitting at my kitchen table, once again staring out into the darkness. The lights of the harbor shimmered on the water. The rising moon cast the mountains to the side of my view with a pearly glow.

My phone vibrated on the table, and my eyes whipped down to the screen.

Fiona: *Blake...*

I wasn't going to leave it at that. I couldn't.

I knew it wasn't smart. I knew that everything we did had to be a secret. But I wanted Fiona. Oh sure, sex was tangled up in it, but that wasn't all. For now, though, I had to shift, adjusting my jeans over the swell of my arousal. Just thinking about her got me aroused.

Lifting my phone, I tapped out another text.

Me: *Do you mind when I call you Fi?*

I didn't even look out the windows this time, staring at the screen. The seconds ticked by before the gray dots appeared, indicating she was replying.

Fiona: *Of course not. It's just a nickname. There's nothing special about it. Other people use it.*

My heart was kicking along. I thought about how she said there was nothing special. I thought about overhearing Tommy call her that the other day. I wasn't a jealous guy. There wasn't any vibe whatsoever between Fiona and any of the guys who worked in the kitchen. Yet I was jealous they were friendly with her. It was beyond irrational, and I damn well knew it.

Me: *Tell me when I can see you again.*

Fiona: *I'm sure you'll see me at work tomorrow.*

I practically growled as I tapped out my response.

Me: *That's not what I mean.*

Fiona: *I don't know how to do this.*

Me: *Tell me your next night off.*

Fiona: *The night after tomorrow.*

Me: *Can I pick you up?*
Fiona: *OMG. No!*
My lips curled in a smile.
Me: *Understood. I'd like to make you dinner. I know you're a mom, though, so maybe getting away for a night isn't an option.*
Fiona: *If I ask, my mom would be thrilled to know I was having dinner with friends.*
Me: *Okay then. 6 o'clock?*
Fiona: *Yes. For the record, I'm not so sure about this.*
Me: *For the record, I understand. I know we're good together. And I know you know that.*
Fiona: *Maybe.*
Me: *I want you. Right, this second. But I'll wait. I just have one question.*
Fiona: *What's that?*
Me: *Are you wet?*
Fiona: *Blake!*
Me: *That's not an answer.*
Fiona: *Good night, Blake.*
Me: *Good night, Fiona.*

Chapter Twenty

FIONA

I set my phone down. My pulse was galloping along, and I felt breathless. For crying out loud, I was lying alone in my bed.

Shifting my legs restlessly, I felt hot all over. Blake's question was on point. I was slippery wet, my arousal leaving my panties damp. I wasn't going to sleep, not unless I did something about it. I slipped my hand between my thighs, past the elastic of my panties and into my swollen, slick folds. I bit my lip to keep from letting out a moan.

Maybe a minute later, I came. Blake's name slipped through my lips in a ragged whisper, unbidden.

I lay there a few minutes later, pleasure

ricocheting in soft pings through my body. I
was in deep.

Chapter Twenty-One

FIONA

The next day, I was at work and had gone into the back to bring some spices forward. I heard footsteps and knew Blake had entered the storage room without even looking. Awareness prickled up my spine, and goosebumps chased over my skin.

I refused to turn around even though I could feel every nerve in my body tingling with awareness. I felt him stop beside me.

"Hey, Fiona," he said, his voice low.

I risked a glance at him and felt heat rise to my cheeks when our eyes collided.

"Hi." My voice came out all breathy.

"I was wondering something," he said, his tone musing.

I licked my lips. "What's that?"

"Did you come last night?"

Heat blazed through me. "Blake!" I hissed.

"I did," he said.

My belly spun in a flip when his lips curled up at one corner, sending tingles through me.

Just then, a server came rushing into the storage room, her eyes landing on us. "Oh, good," she said. "We need more salt and pepper for the tables."

Conveniently, I held a tray with salt and pepper, along with some other spices. "I've got it," I said quickly, stepping past Blake and following her out.

He held a notebook in hand, and I had no idea what she might think of his presence in there. I prayed she thought nothing of it. Fortunately, Blake was always around in the back area.

I flung myself back into the busyness of the evening. I did my best not to think, for even a second, about Blake's naughty question, but it was hard. It broke through again and again, just that one question and his response. His answer nearly burned me up every time I thought of it.

FIONA

"I'm so happy you're meeting some friends." My mother clasped her hands together, squeezing them in front of her chest.

She *really* wanted me to have a social life. I understood why. I wanted one too. More than a relationship, I really did want friends. Getting pregnant in high school didn't make it easy to make friends. I wasn't even talking about the judgment piece, but more that being a single mom just made life wildly busy, so time had been hard to find.

There was also the friction of falling in love with Johnny. Johnny wasn't all bad, not at all. Even now, even after everything had spun out of control for him, my heart pinched whenever I thought of him. He had been good to me.

He had understood why we had to break up. I still believed if he could've seen his own future, he would've made different choices in high school. But when he realized he could make a quick buck by selling his own stimulants, one bad decision snowballed into the next. Like me, his parents had been working class, living paycheck to paycheck. Being able to help them with the bills and help his younger siblings had been way too tempting for him.

There I was, pregnant during my senior year and dating a guy with a risky, rebellious reputation. I hadn't been able to go to college because, well, see the part about being a mom. Johnny hid the snowball effect of his bad decisions until it was too late for me to help.

Not that I was under any illusions that I could've fixed the situation for him and for us and for our daughter, but maybe I could've helped steer him to an exit ramp.

I smiled at my mom, telling myself that I wasn't fully lying. I *was* having dinner with a friend. I had just accidentally added an "s" to that and kept it vague enough that my mom didn't know it was a man, or more specifically

Blake Cannon who I'd fucked in his office the other night at work.

"I'm trying."

"Well, you have a good night." My mom leaned up and kissed my cheek. "We're going to have popcorn and a movie."

"It'll be fun!" Lia exclaimed as she bounced into the kitchen from her bedroom.

I smiled at her, smoothing her hair away from her forehead when she stopped in front of me. "I know you will."

Lia glanced from me to my mother and back again. "I got invited to a slumber party." She bounced on her toes, barely able to contain her excitement. "It's next weekend. Can I go?"

"I need to know who and to check with their parents. It should be okay." I looked up at my mom, who nodded. "You bring home their parents' phone number, and I'll call them."

"I already have it." She reached for her backpack, which hung on a hook above a set of cubbies where she kept her various things. She rummaged through her bag and thrust a piece of paper at me. I glanced down, quickly reading the note. It was definitely neat like an adult's handwriting.

Hi, I'm Donna, Kayla's mom. Kayla would

love to invite Lia over for a slumber party. Please call me. I'm sure you'll want to confirm all the details. Maybe we could set up a playdate. She signed off with her phone number.

My chest tightened. This would be my daughter's first slumber party. She was finally old enough for one. And maybe, just maybe, I could start to make more friends.

I smiled down at Lia, leaning over to press a kiss on the top of her head. "I promise, I'll call her tomorrow."

She bounced up and down before spinning in a circle and racing into her room again.

My mom cast an indulgent smile in the direction of Lia's room before looking back at me. "Go have fun."

"I need to go to the bathroom first." I hurried into the bathroom.

I was nervous and needed one more look at my appearance. While I washed my hands in the sink, I studied myself in the mirror. I still had my hair pulled back, but instead of my usual bun or high ponytail that I wore at work, I had left my hair down with the locks in a tousle around my shoulders. I swiped some lip gloss across my lips.

I experienced a twinge of guilt, knowing I was omitting the details of my dinner with

Blake and who he was. But I didn't feel right telling my mom. She would start asking *way* too many questions about it. She would also wisely tell me I shouldn't do it, that I was risking too much for my job. I told myself I would have dinner with Blake, and this would be it. I would tell him we couldn't keep doing this.

With a last look in the mirror, I hurried out. A short drive later, my phone GPS told me to turn down a side road just a few minutes outside of the downtown area of Fireweed Harbor. I looked around as I drove. I traveled a full mile from one driveway to the next before I saw the address Blake had texted me. Turning down the driveway, I wasn't sure what I expected, but it definitely wasn't what I ended up seeing.

I knew the entire Cannon family was wealthy, seriously wealthy. I had met most of them by now. Even with that knowledge, it was easy to forget their wealth. They were all down-to-earth people who you could imagine were just the usual next-door neighbors.

I guess I expected Blake's house to be fancy. There was absolutely no doubt he had a beautiful piece of property. A glance in my rearview mirror offered a view of the sun setting over the harbor, the sky ablaze with orange and fading rays of gold. His house was nestled into a sloping hill with a view of the mountains to the side. A stream rolled down the side of the slope over a rocky area, complete with a tiny waterfall.

The house itself blended nicely into the landscape. It had wood siding stained a golden hue. The home was tucked into the slope with a deck running the front length of the house. The charcoal gray steel roof peaked at the center, where the windows rose high.

My pulse raced along as I put my car in park. On the whole way here, I'd resisted the urge to turn around and leave. I wanted to see Blake. Too much. I kept trying to convince myself it was the thrill of lust and nothing more. I knew better. There was *so* much more to it, and that revved my anticipation even higher.

I actually liked Blake. He was funny and easygoing, and I felt protected and cared for when I was with him. Every time I thought about our night in his office, the memory on replay was the way I felt after our intense encounter.

After he'd buttoned the last button at the top of my blouse, he'd smoothed his hand down the center, resting it just over the center of my chest. The look in his eyes had held me in place. My heart drummed against his palm. It had felt as if he was protecting it.

I shook that replay away from my thoughts. A moment later, I was cresting the top stair onto the deck when the doorway swung open. "Hi," Blake said simply.

"I didn't even knock!" I blurted out.

"I was waiting."

I had stopped with one foot still on the top stair and the other on the deck.

"Come in." He gestured toward me.

I snapped into motion, catching my foot on the stair as I stumbled forward. Great entrance. Of course.

Blake caught me by the elbow as he took a step to meet me. "Easy there," he murmured.

Tingles scattered through me, and my breath caught when I looked up into his eyes. "Thank you."

He dipped his chin, still holding me by the elbow as he guided me inside. His hand slid around my back to rest on the curve of my waist. The heat of his touch radiated through me as he coaxed me forward.

"This is my place," he said as the door clicked shut behind us.

I paused, glancing around. The entryway

was tiled with windows flanking the front door. There was a coat rack to one side and a small closet to the other. "You can leave your purse here if you want." He pointed at a table by the closet.

"Should I take my shoes off?"

He was wearing socks. "Your call," he replied with a shrug.

Slipping out of my clogs, I set my purse on the table before reaching for my phone and sliding it into my pocket. Glancing up, I said, "Just in case something comes up with Lia."

"You don't need to explain, but that makes sense. How is she?"

I followed him through the archway into an open-concept living room and kitchen area. The living room had a comfy-looking sectional with a large cushioned ottoman and a woodstove tucked in the corner. The windows offered the view of the harbor I'd seen driving in. I could see now that the house had a second story. The upper floor had a balcony with open stairs to one side.

The kitchen sat underneath the balcony area with an island serving as a divider between the living room and kitchen. The hardwood floor shifted to tile.

Blake swung his arm in an arc. "Bedrooms

upstairs, bathroom there if you need it." He gestured to a doorway off to the side. "Would you like something to drink?"

"Just water. I drove so..." My words trailed off as I shrugged.

"Of course."

Something smelled good with salty and sweet scents filling the air. "What's for dinner?"

He walked into the kitchen area, pointing at the island where stools encircled the side by the living room. "Have a seat. I made a potato leek casserole and seared salmon. I promise it's delicious."

"Oh, that sounds good. Do you cook often?" I asked.

I slipped my hips onto one of the stools, leaning into the cushioned back.

"Definitely not as often as you." He got two glasses out of a cabinet by the sink and filled them. "Ice?"

"No, thanks. I've always preferred my water at room temperature."

He slid one of the glasses over to me and got some ice for himself before sitting down across from me. "My mom likes to cook and taught us all. I'm pretty good as far as cooking goes, but nothing like you. When I invited you over, I actually started to get worried and thought maybe I should just get takeout."

I rolled my eyes. "That's silly. I don't cook at home the way I cook for the restaurant." I took a swallow of water, tracing a fingertip in a circle around the glass after I set it down.

He studied me. "I wasn't sure you would actually come tonight."

"All the way until I turned down your driveway, I thought about canceling," I said honestly.

When all he did was watch me quietly, my nerves got the best of me, and I started to blurt out all of my worries. "Blake, I really like you and—" I took a quick breath. "Of course, the other night was—"

Chapter Twenty-Three

FIONA

"Incredible," Blake offered.

My cheeks burned up. "That's one way to put it. You have to understand. My job is really important to me, and I love it."

"I know, and I respect that. I promise no one will know. If it was just sex, I would say screw it. It's not worth the risk. But it's not just sex, not for me."

My heart was beating so hard that I worried I might crack a rib. I took a shaky breath. Before I could think better of it, I replied honestly, "I don't know what to think, but it's not just sex for me either." I took a gulp of water, swallowing quickly before I set the glass down.

Blake's eyes held mine for several beats

before standing and rounding the counter. He stopped beside me, palming my cheek as he brought his lips to mine. His touch was electric, my nerves firing and sending sparks.

His kiss was gentle at first, just a brush of his lips and then another before he angled his head to the side and his tongue swept into my mouth. I let out something between a sigh and a whimper as I arched up to him, our kiss deepening with a blaze of heat sweeping through me.

It was over as quickly as it started. He lifted his head, breaking away and muttering an imprecation. The very air around us was alive and shimmered with electricity.

"I promised you dinner," he said huskily.

I blinked, scrambling for control. I didn't even care about dinner. I just wanted Blake.

I managed to nod. He remained still in front of me, as if undecided. When he glanced down, I discovered my hand was fisted in his shirt, clinging to it. Heat rushed into my cheeks.

With a sheepish smile, I released him. "Can I help with anything?"

Stepping back, he shook his head. "You cook all the time. When I invited you over for dinner, I didn't want you to work."

"I actually like to cook." My voice was a little breathless.

His lips kicked up at one corner when he glanced back as he stopped in front of the stove. "I know you do. I made sure to have almost everything done before you got here just so you wouldn't feel like you needed to help."

I grinned. "Smart man."

His chuckle sent goosebumps prickling over the surface of my skin. *This* man. He made me crazy in ways I never imagined.

I liked Blake. I *really* liked him. It was reckless beyond measure. More than that, I was in thrall to him, awash in desire and need. I had the worst kind of crush on him. I couldn't even remember having this kind of crush on a guy. I tried to think back to when I was crushing on Johnny in high school. When I was young and foolish and didn't know better. Back then, I was so young it was easy to like a guy. Johnny was my first real boyfriend.

I knew better now, so much better. Ever since I'd had Lia, I'd thought myself well over crushing on any man. Having a baby would do that to you. And now, steeped in the cynicism of watching a young man I'd loved, make too many reckless decisions that drew him down a path he couldn't veer away from, I'd believed myself immune to falling for anyone.

Until Blake.

He moved about his kitchen with efficiency. It was a really nice kitchen too.

"I have a crush on your kitchen," I offered as he slid a casserole pan out of the oven. The gleaming stainless-steel oven was built into the wall directly beside a stove top with six burners, including a double burner in the center.

"A crush on my kitchen?" He turned and set the pan on two trivets conveniently placed beside the oven.

I swung my arm in an arc. "Of course! You've got a top-of-the-line oven and stove top with a refrigerator to match. But more than that, it's the flow."

"Flow?" he prompted as he turned and quickly removed the salmon from under the broiler.

"Yes, with the island here and a sink built into this, along with a larger sink over there. You have plenty of space between there and the island. It would be easy for more than one person to be in here doing things. I'm sure you had someone design it for you."

Blake held my gaze for a beat. "I did and just went with what she recommended."

"Like I said, I have a crush on your kitchen."

It was much safer to crush on his kitchen than him. A few minutes later, I took a bite of the salmon, letting out a moan as the mingled flavors of the rich fish with a parmesan crust and lemon and butter burst across my tongue. "Excellent," I announced when I finished chewing.

Blake flashed a grin while he chewed, and my belly spun in a flip.

Chapter Twenty-Four

BLAKE

Note to self: watching Fiona eat made me crazy.

She let out these little moans of satisfaction, and I was hard the entire time. It was enough to drive me to distraction. I had picked up dessert from The Sugar Spoon.

Fiona bit her lip as she smiled down at the plate. "I haven't had a chance to get anything from there yet. I've heard about it."

I waggled my brows as I grinned over at her. "It's not right in town. It's sort of hidden."

"Where exactly is it?" she inquired.

"Only about five minutes outside of downtown proper. An elderly couple started it in their house. Their granddaughter is taking it over, but it's still at their house. They transformed their garage into the bakery. It's not cheap to get anything from there."

Fiona twisted her lips, nodding. "That's what I heard. It's part of why I haven't gone out of my way to find it yet. Being a single mom means money is usually tight."

I didn't like knowing she worried about money. "Have a bite." I gestured to it.

She sank her fork into the cheesecake, lifting it to her lips. As her mouth closed around the fork and she let out a satisfied moan, my cock swelled even further. I gritted my teeth, shifting in my seat. Fuck me. I usually had more control.

"Oh wow," she enthused when she finished chewing. "This is amazing. Just getting the texture right so it's not too heavy is challenging with cheesecake. This is light and fluffy. I'll need to find it. I want to get something for my mom and Lia."

"I'll take you there. We should bring Lia out there with us. They have a whole kids' display case."

By a damn miracle, I willed my arousal to half-mast by the time we finished eating dessert.

Fiona insisted on helping me clean up, wagging her finger at me when I tried to protest. "Don't even. I'm helping. You made dinner."

She worked quickly and efficiently, loading the dishwasher after allowing me to rinse the dishes in the sink. Once she wiped the counter and hung up the dish towel after drying her hands, she turned, resting her hips against the counter.

"Thank you." Her voice was quiet.

She stood by the island, and I was across from her by the sink. I idly thought to myself that she was too far away. I needed to be closer to her. I could feel the voltage reverberating in the space between us.

"You're welcome," I belatedly replied. "What time do you need to go home?"

She blinked before glancing down at her watch. "In an hour." My system sizzled with a jolt when her lashes lifted and her eyes met mine again. Fuck me. *This woman.*

I needed to make sure I didn't push her too far, too fast. I held my hand out. "Come here."

She was quiet for several thundering beats of my heart before she stepped away from the counter, taking one step and curling her hand into mine. I tugged her lightly. She took another step as I reeled her closer to me.

Her eyes searched mine before she whispered, "I can't think when I'm this close to you."

"Then don't."

Releasing her hand, I slid my palm around her waist, bringing her flush against me. She let out a soft, surprised yelp.

Lifting my other hand, I slid my fingers through her silky locks. "I like your hair down," I rasped.

"You do?"

"I do. I like it up too. Because then, I can imagine... This." I punctuated my words with a kiss as I laced my fingers into her hair. It was thick and luxurious.

Our kiss went deep quickly as her tongue glided out to tease against mine. I angled her head to the side, letting my palm slide around to cup her nape. I couldn't get enough of her. I took deep sips of her, savoring the taste of her, the smell of her, and the feel of her plush lips.

We broke apart, the sound of our ragged breath filling the air. Fiona's eyes were dark, almost navy, and when she looked up at me, her lips were kiss swollen. She reached between us, pressing her palm over my throbbing arousal.

"Fuck, Fiona," I bit out.

She stepped back, and my hand fell away from her waist. "I need to do this," she whispered.

Before I could even think, she swiftly unbuttoned my jeans and slid her palm into my boxers. I let out something between a growl and a groan when I felt her hand curl around my cock. She shoved my jeans down a little, her eyes on mine. Her touch slid up and down, gripping lightly.

"Fiona," I said, almost a warning.

She bit her lip, a naughty glint in her gaze. Her lips curled at one corner. "You just wait," she teased before she leaned over and swirled her tongue around the end of my cock.

I felt a drop of cum slip out the tip into her mouth as she sucked me in deeply. I gripped the edge of the counter with one hand and her hair with the other.

Holy hell. Feeling her suck my length into her mouth nearly brought me to the edge instantly.

I held on to that counter as if my very life depended on it while she teased me to distraction, drawing me in deeply. The suction alone pushed my release closer and closer. I felt my balls drawing up tightly, and everything in me sizzled as I teetered on the edge of my control. She dragged her tongue along the underside of my cock.

I looked down to see her angling to look up at me. At the mere sight of her wet lips and her tongue swirling around my thick crown, another spurt of cum rolled out. I wanted to be inside her. I *needed* to be inside her when I let go.

"Fiona," I bit out. "I need—"

"What do you need, Blake?" She rocked back on her heels as she peered up at me.

I hauled her up, tugging at her clothes. Blessedly, she helped, shimmying out of her jeans quickly. I yanked at her blouse. I needed her bare skin against mine. A moment later, I was lifting her hips onto the counter.

Fiona made this sexy fucking sound in the back of her throat, a little hitch of her breath followed by a pleading whimper. I stilled for a moment, bringing my eyes to meet hers. We stared at each other.

While we were caught in a storm of need and passion, a sense of intimacy bloomed in the air between us. It felt as if my own heart was linked to hers, silken ribbons tightening with every beat.

I stepped closer and curled my hands around her hips, tugging her to the edge of the counter. Somewhere in the heated rush of getting her undressed, she had yanked at the buttons of my shirt. I hadn't even noticed it until her palm landed slightly off-center on my chest, just over my heart.

My heart crashed against my ribs as if reaching for her touch. I released her hip, my palms sliding along the insides of her thighs to push her knees apart. Her skin was silky and soft. Her eyes held mine, and I could barely catch my breath. I broke free from the intensity of her gaze to let my eyes dip down, taking in the plump curves of her breasts and the blush covering her skin. My eyes dipped further down to land on her pink pussy, glistening from her arousal.

I couldn't help it. I *had* to touch her. I slid my palm farther up her thigh, teasing my fingers into her swollen folds. She let out a soft whimper as her hips rocked into my touch. I leaned down, bringing my mouth to her sex. Because I had to taste her. She was sweet and salty.

Her hands curled around the edges of the counter as I licked deeply into her before dragging my tongue up and around her clit. Just once. Only once.

I needed to feel her fly apart around me. When I straightened, our gazes caught again. I stepped toward her, curling my palm around my length as I tugged her just a little closer to the edge of the counter.

Dragging my cock through her slippery folds, I watched when she bit her lip and let out a ragged moan. My release threatened, lightning sizzling down my spine and into my balls as they tightened and drew up.

I teased her yet again, dragging my cock down and back up to slide over her swollen bud. At the last second, sanity broke through the haze of lust obliterating my thoughts.

"Fuck!" I stepped back quickly. "I need a condom."

Fiona reached for me, her fingers curling around the hem of my shirt. "I'm on birth control. We don't need to worry about anything, not from me."

I stared at her. "I always use a condom." Which was true. I had never had sex without a condom.

I trusted Fiona. Completely.

"Please don't make me wait," she rasped.

Because I was in thrall to Fiona, to my need, to this thrumming intimacy, all I could do was answer her plea.

I stepped closer, once again gripping my

cock and notching it at her entrance. Releasing myself, I shifted closer yet again, sliding my hand around her waist to rest at the base of her spine. I held her gaze as I took a breath and thrust once. I seated myself deeply with a single swift surge.

She cried out, her eyes falling closed. I could already feel her clenching and rippling around me. I was barely, just barely, clinging to the edge of my control, as if gripping the side of a cliff with my fingertips, about to fall at any second.

I held still for several beats of my heart before letting my forehead fall to hers. "Come for me, sweetheart." My lips moved against hers with every word.

I drew back and thrust inside her again, and then again just as I brought my fingers between us and teased over her plump clit. She cried out, her pussy clenching. My name followed in a ragged breath as her entire body went taut before she shuddered all over.

My voice was slurred, nearly drunk on the feel of being bare inside her. She was silky slick and warm.

My release came on the heels of another breath as I nudged just a little deeper inside her. It was fierce and hard, whipsawing through me and yanking my breath out of me. I chanted her name over and over.

She went soft, curling against me with her head tucking into my shoulder as I held her close. I was stunned at the force of my release and how it felt to be this close to her.

Chapter Twenty-Five

FIONA

I wanted to stay here forever. Blake's heartbeat was strong and steady against my ear where it rested just below his collarbone. I savored the way his fingers sifted through the ends of my hair. I barely remembered the order of events.

Somehow, I was mostly naked with my shirt hanging off one shoulder. His palm smoothed down my back, the calloused surface sending a prickly sensation over my skin.

I didn't want to think, and I didn't know what to think. Everything with Blake felt, simply put, amazing. Yet I also felt raw and unguarded. I'd only been with one other man, Johnny. It had been sweet with him. I had left our relationship when I was young and not fully formed as a person yet.

Now, I felt older and more cynical, deeply untrusting in some ways. Not because Johnny had broken my heart that way. He'd been faithful to me. He'd broken my heart because he had let me down with his reckless decisions that led him somewhere I never could've imagined.

After him, I just couldn't let my guard down with anyone. And so *this*, this wild, thrumming, out-of-control reckless need I felt for Blake muddled all my thoughts. I couldn't imagine being this vulnerable with anyone. Yet on a level beyond intellect, I trusted Blake completely.

I just didn't trust myself or the universe.

I took several steadying breaths as my body started to settle, swirling eddies of need and passion beginning to slow as I caught my breath. Eventually, I lifted my head oh-so reluctantly. I was almost afraid to look into Blake's eyes. Not because I feared him or what he might think, but because it was all too intimate. All too much.

I took a deep breath before steeling myself and opening my eyes. He was right there waiting, his silvery grays snagging mine. I felt as if he was peering deep into my heart, past my anxious confusion. As if he could see the "me" I didn't share with anyone.

He was quiet as he studied me, and I looked right back at him. He lifted one of his hands to smooth my hair away from my cheek. "Well."

My chirping phone snapped through the moment. His hand fell away before he leaned forward to brush his lips over mine. It felt as if a flame had passed between us.

When he stepped away for a moment, I felt bereft, instantly missing the depth of our connection, the physical closeness.

"Do you need to get that?" he asked.

My heart twinged a little. He knew my daughter was home with my mom, and maybe they needed me.

"I can check in a minute."

He helped me off the counter and we put our clothing back to rights. Only then did I cross over to where my phone sat on the table.

I glanced at the unknown number on the screen. It could've just been spam. The world was filled with spam phone calls. But there was a message. Ever since I had gotten a message from another unknown number, I was anxious. I tapped the screen to check my voicemail. The transcription filled quickly, and it was that same guy, Gerald. I distantly recalled Johnny had a friend with that name in high school. I hadn't known him well.

Blake must've sensed something, or maybe my expression revealed my anxiety. I heard his footsteps approaching. He stopped beside me, his palm landing between my shoulder blades, his touch warm and comforting.

"What is it?" he asked gently.

The moment I met his gaze, the concern there so evident, a sob escaped. The next thing I knew, I burst into tears.

"Hey, hey," Blake said.

He took my phone from my hand, pressing the button on the side to close it before he set it on the table. He pulled me into his arms. His embrace was warm, solid, and everything I needed at this moment.

The rush of tears ran out quickly. I was utterly mortified. I kept my face pressed into his chest as his hand moved in soothing passes up and down my back.

"Look at me." I heard the rumble of his voice against my ear.

I didn't want to look up because then I would have to explain. Maybe I didn't have to explain, but I was afraid and needed to tell someone.

I reluctantly lifted my head and blurted out the truth. "Lia's father died. He was a good guy, but he died two years ago. Everything went wrong before then because he started dealing stimulants in high school. He got in over his head, and he kept doing it. We broke up before he died. He still took care of us financially. I just needed to get out of there, out of that situation. I was getting by in Seattle, but Seattle is really expensive. When I got this job up here, it was perfect. But this guy's left two messages saying I need to stay quiet, and I don't know what to do. I don't know what he's talking about."

Blake studied me quietly before he cupped my cheeks, kissing me fiercely. "It'll be okay. We'll just file a report with the police. I'll go with you."

"I don't think it's that simple," I said.

"He's dead, and you don't know what this guy is talking about. I'm sorry he died, for you and for Lia, but it's not okay to call someone and threaten them. We'll make it right."

I stared at him for a long moment before taking a shaky breath. "I don't know if it's that easy, but I think you're right. We have to start somewhere." I bit my lip. "You probably think I'm an idiot."

He shook his head decisively. "You're not responsible for the choices your ex made. And, Lord knows, nobody's past is perfect. My family's got more than enough skeletons in the closet. Trust me on that."

Because I tended to keep to myself, I didn't know the whole story of the Cannon family, but I knew they had a complicated history. Even then, I suppose all families did, one way or another. Now didn't seem the time to pry. I swallowed. "Thanks for understanding."

"Did you actually think I would judge you for something your boyfriend from high school did?"

I shrugged. "I assume most people would. I had a baby with him. I really didn't know how bad things had gotten until it was too late. I still believe he was a good man. He just took a few wrong turns."

Blake nodded slowly. "I can understand that. For what it's worth, if we were all judged for the way we were in high school—" He paused and rolled his eyes, letting out a dry chuckle. "The world would be a mess."

I couldn't help myself. "I screwed up big-time because I got pregnant. But what did you do?"

"For starters, I don't think you screwed

up. Lia is adorable, and it's clear you're a good mom. As to your question, I got into some pretty big trouble for drag racing." He shrugged sheepishly.

"Drag racing?!"

"I like to drive fast. A group of us used to get together and race on the deserted roads along the edge of town. Drive fast, take chances, and all that. Car insurance for young men is so much more expensive for a reason."

I couldn't help but giggle. "That doesn't seem so bad."

Blake shrugged before he leaned down and pressed a quick kiss on my lips. "Maybe, maybe not. But we also bet on it, and we got in trouble. I definitely should've lost my license, but I got by with a warning."

I wanted to reach for his hand and pull him back to me, but I knew it was just about time for me to get home. "I guess it seems like what I did was much bigger. I had a baby, and Johnny—he was my ex—got into a lot more trouble. His parents didn't have much money, and neither did mine. When he realized he could sell his own stimulants to make extra cash, he did. Before I knew it, that was basically his job."

"How did he die?" Blake asked gently.

My heart burned a little. "An accidental

overdose. He got a little too comfortable with drugs. He didn't use many, but I guess he didn't know not to combine certain ones. He had a reaction, and he died. And now, Lia doesn't have her father, who she adored, and I've got some guy I don't even know calling me and telling me to stay quiet."

"I'll go to the police station with you to file the report."

I shook my head quickly. "No. That might seem weird." I gestured back and forth between us. "I shouldn't even be here."

It abruptly hit me just how deep I had gotten in this entanglement with Blake.

He stepped closer to me, lifting his knuckles and nudging my chin up. "You should be here. I meant what I said, though. If you don't want anyone to know, no one will know. But you're not some dirty secret to me."

Chapter Twenty-Six

FIONA

You're not some dirty secret to me.

Blake's words played on repeat in my mind a few mornings later in the shower. When I got home that night, I was so relieved my mom had been asleep. If not, she would've asked me *about dinner, my friends,* and so on. I preferred to keep my lying to a minimum.

In this case, I was lying by omission and leaving out massive swaths of information, specifically the gender and name of my friend, and most definitely avoiding the kernel of information that it was Blake Cannon. Even worse, I was getting hot and heavy with him. I didn't usually hide things from my mom. Even with Johnny, I hadn't considered myself reckless, but I suppose it might have seemed that way from the outside. Getting pregnant had genuinely been an accident. We'd been careful and used condoms.

I thought about Johnny for a few moments. It felt different with Blake. Everything with Johnny had been a first. First kiss, first everything. I carried so much shame about how things turned out for him, but I didn't even blame him. His parents needed the money. The income he'd brought in had made a true difference for that family. But it got messy. *Really* messy.

Johnny had taught me the lesson that no person was all good or bad. There were so many shades of gray. In the eyes of the law, I knew he had been a criminal because he illegally sold controlled substances. Yet he was a good man to me, to our daughter, and to his family. I knew some people who never broke the law on paper and were horrible to the people they allegedly cared about.

I let out a little sigh as I finished rinsing my hair, then quickly dried off and got dressed. Lia was already off at school, and I had three hours before I needed to go into the restaurant. I was nervous, but I braced myself to tell my mother what was happening with the voice messages.

Walking out into the kitchen area, I called, "Morning, Mom."

She smiled over at me from where she sat at the table doing her daily crossword. "Good morning, dear. Coffee is ready." She bowed her head, penciling in another answer on her puzzle.

I filled my mug with coffee and added a little bit of cream. A moment later, I slipped into the chair across from her. "Thanks for making the coffee."

"Always."

I took a sip, contemplating how to start this conversation. Because my mother was a mind reader, she nudged me along. "Something's on your mind. It has been for days."

I laughed as I looked over at her. My stomach churned with anxiety, but my mother knew me well. This had been on my mind for too many days, ever since that first phone message.

After a fortifying swallow of coffee, I set the mug down, tracing my thumb along the handle as I looked over at her. "I had a message on my phone and then another one from Gerald, who said he worked with Johnny. He said he didn't know who I talked to and told me I needed to stay quiet. Obviously, I don't know what he's talking about. I'm going to talk to the police about it today." I tried to say all of that as calmly as I possibly could.

My mother's eyes narrowed, and she pressed her lips in a line. "Who is Gerald?"

You would've thought Gerald had seriously done my mother wrong in another life from the way she spat his name out.

"The only thing I know about Gerald is he left me two messages. I think Johnny was friends with a guy named Gerald in high school. That's all I know." I let out a quick sigh. "I swear, I don't know anything else."

"Have you told anyone about this? Why do you want to call the police?"

"Because I had nothing to do with any of this! I didn't talk to anyone and don't even know what I'm supposed to keep quiet. Johnny and I weren't even together the last two years before he died. I feel like if I don't report it, he's just gonna keep calling me."

"How did he even get your number?" my mother pressed.

"I don't know, Mom, but I have nothing to hide. I wasn't involved in Johnny's 'business.'" I added air quotes for emphasis.

My heart ached. I missed Johnny. He wasn't bad, and I knew he loved Lia and me.

"Mom, you can't think I'll just let these messages keep coming and not do anything?"

My mother shook her head as she let out a huff. When my mom was worried, she got angry. She was a fierce mama-bear kind of personality, which I completely understood. That was how I was with my daughter. That was why I broke up with Johnny, as much as it tore me up to do it.

"Fine. You should call the police. Would you like me to go with you?"

"Actually, I would."

Relief gusted through me. It would feel better not to do it alone.

"Also, don't forget I clean the police station on the weekends. I know some of them. The chief of police is a very nice guy. Very nice."

For a split second, I thought I saw a blush on my mom's cheeks. "Very nice?" I cocked my head to the side. "Sounds like you know him pretty well, Mom."

She rolled her eyes. "He's just a good man. Plus, you know I like a man in uniform."

My dad had been a police officer. That added to my guilt about what Johnny ended up doing. My dad was so disappointed because he'd actually liked Johnny.

I chuckled. "I know you do. When should we go?" I glanced at my watch. "I have two hours and forty-eight minutes before I need to be at the restaurant for my shift. Do you have any cleaning jobs today?"

"Just Clara Cannon, but that schedule is flexible. I don't usually go until the afternoon anyway," she replied.

"You're cleaning the Cannons' house?"

This was news to me. It's not like I had a running tally of who my mom cleaned for.

"There's more than one Cannon. For crying out loud, that woman had eight children."

"I thought there were seven," I countered.

My mother's brow furrowed. "Her eldest died. It's very sad."

"Oh! That's terrible."

Questions tumbled through my thoughts. If I got too nosy about the Cannons with my mother, she would know something was up. I couldn't help but think of Blake's comment that he had his own complicated family history.

"I can't believe you haven't heard that," my mother said as she stood from the table and closed her crossword book.

"I try not to get too caught up in gossip," I replied.

"But their family owns the restaurant where you work," she pointed out.

"David is the one who runs it, and he doesn't gossip, certainly not to me."

My mother watched as I drained my coffee quickly and stood from the table. "Not all gossip is bad. In small towns, it's best to stay up to speed. Otherwise, you can get caught flat-footed. You have to at least know who the assholes are."

"I'm pretty sure the Cannons aren't the assholes in town." I rinsed my cup in the sink.

My mother took it from me and put it in the dishwasher. Dishes were never left in our sink. She wouldn't abide by it.

"Oh, they're definitely not the assholes. I don't know them all, but I think I've met—" My mom counted on her fingers. "Rhys, Blake, McKenna, Adam, and Kenan. I still haven't met Wyatt or Griffin. They live out of town, though. I met most of them when I was at Clara's place."

I stared at my mother, my mouth dropping open. "Are you besties with Clara Cannon? Maybe I don't have all the gossip in Fireweed Harbor, but I know the Cannons are the equivalent of royalty here."

My mother grinned. "Perhaps they are, but they're also very nice people and down to earth. They didn't always have money. Clara is a sweetheart."

"I guess I'll just come to you when I need some news," I teased as we walked toward the doorway.

My mother waggled her brows. "Maybe you should."

Chapter Twenty-Seven

FIONA

"This is my daughter, Fiona!" My mother curled her fingers into my sleeve, shaking me as if she was holding up a piece of paper. I suppose I was truly her creation. Sometimes her pride could be a bit much.

I smiled at the man standing in front of us as I shook his hand. "Hi, Fiona," he said warmly. "I'm Mike Taylor, the chief of police here in Fireweed Harbor. I hear you have a matter to discuss?"

"I do. Would it be possible for us to meet for a few minutes?" I was a bundle of jittery nerves.

"Of course. Come on back." He gestured for us to follow him down a hallway.

When we sat down in his office, I began with, "Chief—"

He shook his head quickly. "Feel free to just call me Mike. Everybody in town calls me Mike, and I consider your mother a friend."

"Okay, Mike." I took a breath, bracing myself. "My daughter's father, who passed away two years ago, was involved in—"

My mother cut in. "Dealing drugs," she said matter-of-factly. "Fiona didn't know. Well, after she found out, they broke up. Johnny was actually a good man, but he made some poor choices."

Mike's eyes didn't hold even a flicker of judgment. He simply nodded. "So if Johnny passed away, then..."

"I had no involvement in what he was doing. None." I held my hands up. "But in the past few weeks, I've gotten two messages from a man named Gerald telling me he doesn't know who I talked to and I need to stay quiet. I haven't talked to anyone and don't even know what he thinks I need to hide. I did cooperate with the police when Johnny got in trouble before he died. I don't even know how Gerald tracked me down because I don't have the same cell number from when I lived in Seattle. My boss at the restaurant I worked for in Seattle there is good friends with David at Fireweed Winery."

"Of course. I know David. Do you still have the messages?" Mike asked.

Mike had me play the messages and forward them to him. He made notes before looking over at me. "While he hasn't made any direct threats, he's implying you know something he wants you to keep quiet. You clearly do not. Was your daughter's father legally charged?"

"Once. I'm actually the one who reported him." I still had mixed feelings about that because it seemed like that was what unraveled everything for Johnny. Even then, he'd never held it against me.

Mike tapped his fingers on his desk. "I'd like to put a call in to the police in Seattle if you don't mind. They might be able to get us a lead on this Gerald guy and let him know he needs to leave you alone."

I took a breath, the bands of tension around my chest loosening slightly for the first time in weeks. "Do you think I need to be worried he'll do something?"

Mike kept drumming his fingertips on his desk. "I would like to tell you he won't, but I don't really know how deep into the situation your daughter's father was and what this guy is worried about. Even if your ex owed money at the time he died, it's not your responsibility. Once people believe they can bully someone, they keep doing it."

I didn't realize how tightly my fingers were laced together until I let out a breath. I stretched my hands.

"Fireweed Harbor is a small town. People can't just roll in here and not be noticed. I think you and your daughter will be safe. We just need to nip this situation in the bud." Mike looked toward my mother. "I'm really glad you encouraged your daughter to let me know what was going on."

"I knew you would help." My mother beamed at Mike, and his eyes crinkled at the corners with a warm smile. I was pretty sure they had a mutual crush, but I wasn't about to get into my mother's love life.

A few minutes later when we stood to leave, Mike smiled over at me. "Very nice to meet you, Fiona. Please let me know if you get any more messages or if anything unusual happens." He handed me a business card with his phone number. "Put that number in your phone. That's my direct cell number."

When we climbed in the car, my mother smiled over at me. "There. I told you Mike would take care of it."

"I'm just hoping I don't hear from this guy again. That's all I want."

Chapter Twenty-Eight

BLAKE

Quinn Blackthorn eyed me over the top of her glasses. "Blake, you're a helpful guy, and I know you help out plenty of your employees, as does Rhys."

"Yeah, we try to treat our staff well."

Quinn smiled. "You do. I love that Fireweed Industries is a family-oriented company. You also treat your employees really well where it matters, as far as benefits. But I digress." She cocked her head to the side, her gaze considering. "Whatever is going on with Fiona, it seems like it might be more than helping your average employee."

Fortunately, I was fairly skilled at playing it cool, so I simply arched a brow and ignored the way my heart tumbled a little in my chest. "She let me know about a concern, and I suggested she let the police know. I didn't know if you had any additional recommendations," I said.

Quinn nodded. "Of course. I would suggest she follow any recommendations the police have. In the meantime, if something else is going on, please be aware that it'll be more of a problem for her than you. I'm not talking about employment consequences." She wrinkled her nose. "Public opinions can be brutal and hard to escape in a small town."

Chapter Twenty-Nine

BLAKE

Public opinions can be brutal and hard to escape in a small town.

Quinn's observation, uncomfortably spot-on, repeated in my thoughts over the following days. I couldn't help but wonder if I'd made a mistake in letting myself give in to the desire I felt for Fiona.

Yet every time doubts began to crowd my thoughts, my heart thrashed in my chest. I knew what plain old lust was. My desire for Fiona was fierce, yet that wasn't all I felt for her. Not by a long shot.

Work was busy. Always. I felt as if my body were an antenna, constantly attuned to the frequency of Fiona. I knew when she was in the building even though the restaurant was on the other side of our production complex with my office down a long hallway, past the bottling area.

I found myself checking on things closer to the other side of the building more than I usually would. I tried to tell myself that it wasn't just because I wanted to catch a glimpse of her. I had plenty of reasons to check on various issues.

My primary involvement in the restaurant was hosting the weekly tastings. The locals loved these. We kept them going to maintain a strong connection to the roots of what became Fireweed Industries. The winery and brewery started it all. Of course, we also made money hand over fist at them even though we gave away plenty of alcohol. People stayed for more than the initial free drink and crowded the restaurant for dinner because we offered special prices to the locals during those events.

I told myself to remember what Quinn said as I strolled down the hallway to make my way into the event room we used for the tastings. We had a gift store where we sold local art, jewelry, and so on. It was also for the winery and brewery, the only retail location for our alcohol sales as the rest were sold through distributors to places throughout the country.

I didn't need to take a detour to get something from the break room. I reminded myself I was friendly with lots of staff, which was entirely accurate.

The second I walked in, I didn't even have to look to know Fiona was in the room. Every hair on my body stood on end, and awareness prickled down my spine. I glanced around, my gaze encompassing the room in a quick arc. My eyes landed on Fiona. Her back was to me as she looked down at something. Her outfit wasn't remarkable—a skirt that fell below her knees and a blouse tucked in the waist. Her hair was tied up in a bun with a few loose tendrils dangling down the back of her neck.

I wanted to cross the room, stop behind her, slide my arms around her waist, and dip my head to press hot kisses along the back of her neck. My mouth watered. Because I knew how she tasted. I knew her scent.

"Blake!" Norma Jackson said.

Her voice broke through the haze beginning to cloud my thoughts, and I glanced over. "Hey there, Norma. How are you?"

"Doing just fine. I wanted to thank you

for helping my son with his flat tire the other day."

"You don't need to thank me for that. I'd stop and help anyone with a flat tire," I replied.

She stopped beside me. "You're a good man." She patted me on the elbow, her air warm and motherly. "Where are you headed?"

I glanced at my watch. "Countdown to the rush in about ten minutes." It suddenly occurred to me that I needed a reason to be walking through here. "Bathroom break first."

"See you out front," Norma replied. Norma had worked for us for as long as I could remember. She'd done various tasks and was familiar enough with all of our operations that she could help out almost anywhere in a pinch. On tasting nights, she usually worked the bar and helped out with cleanup at the end of the busy nights.

I walked toward the bathroom, which happened to be near where Fiona's locker was. She glanced up, and our eyes met. I could feel the electricity sizzling in the air between us.

Not trusting myself to speak, I simply dipped my chin in acknowledgment and slipped into the bathroom. My heartbeat was thundering. I stayed there long enough to realistically go to the bathroom, then let the cold water run over my hands longer than necessary to quell the heat rising swiftly inside my body.

I was disappointed when I stepped out, and Fiona wasn't there. That was how bad I had it for her. I craved every glimpse of her.

BLAKE

"Busy tonight?" Rhys asked as he approached. He stopped by the corner of the bar against the wall.

"Always," I replied. "Where's Haven?"

"She's working late with McKenna."

I chuckled. "How is that going?"

Stopping across from him, I glanced toward Norma to see if she needed anything. Her hands flew while she filled a pint glass with one hand and passed over two bottles with the other.

When I met Rhys's eyes again, he grinned. "It's going well. Haven's schedule is actually better than it was before. When she was working full-time at the café and doing her online stuff, she might've been home more often, but she was working when she was home. She still fills in at the café when they need extra help, but her evenings are usually free. She and McKenna are working on the graphics for some publicity campaign for the rollout in Willow Brook."

Fireweed Industries had recently reconfigured an entire operation in Willow Brook, Alaska, where we had previously run a mine. Our cousin Archer, along with our half-brother Chase, had been working together to transition it into a renewable energy business. They were finally ready to open it officially.

"Ah, that's right. Are any of us going down there for the opening? Also, would you like a beer?" At Rhys's nod, I handed him our latest limited-edition run of blackberry coffee beer.

He took a swallow, nodding in appreciation before he replied, "I'm going down there. Haven and McKenna will be with me. I believe Kenan and Adam are planning to go. I'm not sure about Wyatt and Griffin."

"I'll text Wyatt. You never know."

"Wyatt actually called me the other day," Rhys added.

"Seriously?"

Rhys nodded. "Yeah, just checking on

that boat he bought. He stays in touch, even if it isn't that frequent."

Haven slipped between a group of people standing behind Rhys and sidled up to him at the bar. She smiled up at him. "Hey." My older brother's gaze softened, and he gave her a lingering kiss.

Her cheeks were pink when she glanced over at me a moment later. "Hi, Blake. Busy tonight."

"That's always our goal. Anything for you?"

"Just water," Haven replied.

I still couldn't believe Haven was pregnant, but I was happy for her and Rhys. Once he'd adjusted to the news, he'd been thrilled.

I was handing Haven her glass of water a moment later when McKenna arrived. "Hey!" She leaned across the bar, lifting her hand for a high five. After I slapped my palm against hers, I asked, "What'll it be?"

"Whatever the new seasonal mead is. I'm in the mood for something a little fruity."

"Coming right up. This week, we've got a new batch of blackberry," I replied. "I hear you're keeping Haven late."

"Just because we've got the big opening soon. Will you be there?" McKenna asked.

"I'm sure I can make it. As long as it's not scheduled when I have a tasting."

"These things pretty much run themselves," McKenna replied. "It's on a Friday, so that should work."

"That'll work. Are you guys flying or taking the ferry?"

"Flying," Rhys said succinctly. "Much as I love the ferry trip, we don't have time."

"And we're flying commercial," McKenna interjected pointedly. "In fact, we're selling the private plane."

My brows hitched up. None of us used it much, but we owned it. "No worries on my end, but what's the point?"

"Pay attention to the news. Rich people with private planes are spewing gobs of pollution into the atmosphere. It's embarrassing. Since we're committed to making Fireweed Industries a leader in environmentally sound business investments and practices, we have to make some personal changes," my sister explained.

"I agree, but commercial flights send plenty of pollution into the atmosphere," I replied.

McKenna rolled her eyes.

Kenan arrived, followed by Adam. They all lingered over in that corner by the bar. At one point, I dipped into the back and wondered if I could send Fiona a text. I knew it was her late night. I shouldn't even care about her schedule, but I did. I slipped my phone out.

Me: *You're working late tonight. No pressure, but if you wanted to see me, just reply. I'll find you in the back storage area.*

My heartbeat kicked a little faster as soon as I hit send. Fuck me. I didn't think Fiona realized just how much I wanted her. When I returned to the front, I was swept into a busy stretch.

The last hour or so crawled by for me. The entire time, my attention was half focused on whether Fiona would reply. When I finally felt my phone vibrate in my pocket, I checked it to see her response.

Fiona: *Ok.*

That was it, but it was enough to rev the engine of my need.

Chapter Thirty-One

FIONA

I pushed through the double-wide swinging doors into the back hallway that led to the production area. Even though the kitchen area for the restaurant was quiet now, the cacophony of the customers in the bar area could still be heard. It was muted when the doors swung shut behind me.

The first portion of this hallway had doorways leading to the storage areas for the restaurant. Beyond that was another set of swinging doors that led to production and distribution. There was a large warehouse at the end of that next stretch of hallway with a few offices along the way, including Blake's.

My pulse cantered along and picked up to

a gallop as I slipped into the dry storage area. I held a notebook in my hand, the one I used to keep track of what we needed for the next day. I had already been back here once and gotten everything prepped. If anyone happened to come along before Blake, I had an excuse.

Just thinking about Blake sent fiery pinwheels of heat through me. I knew this wasn't sensible. It was the opposite of sensible. It was reckless, and careless, and had the potential to do more than ruin my career here. I also knew Blake could break my heart.

Yet my heart was driving this recklessness. I wanted to blame it on lust, and we had plenty of that. The chemistry between us was a force I couldn't contain. After years of trying to make good decisions, to walk that narrow path, no wider than a balance beam, where no one could question my choices, I stumbled and lost my balance. Being a young mother came with many downfalls. My daughter made up for all of them in spades. My love for her was bigger than anything I ever could've imagined. But I knew the way people looked at me. I was usually much younger than most mothers waiting at the school drop-off. I was young enough that people could confuse my mother for being my daughter's mother rather than her grandmother.

It was all worth it. I tried so hard never to make another reckless choice. I hadn't even dated since Johnny and I broke up, not even once. I hadn't wanted to. I was busy and usually running on fumes. I couldn't even imagine how tired I would've been without my mother helping me. As it was, most days felt like a long country mile over bumpy dirt roads, and I was exhausted and weary at the end.

Knowing all that was at stake, here I was, walking into the back, hoping this man I was falling for so hard and fast would be there. It felt like I was skydiving and hadn't pulled the cord yet. I could only hope I wouldn't crash land.

My need to see Blake bordered on desperation. Knowing that his family owned the place where I worked only amped up my need. Not because I wanted the money or anything. I didn't care about that. It felt naughty, forbidden. *That* had my body flush with arousal.

If a full minute passed after I stepped into the storage room, I would've been shocked. I sensed Blake before I heard him. Every cell on my body fired sparks. I forced myself not to turn around, just in case I was wrong and it was someone else. I wasn't wrong.

Another second later, I felt him behind me. The hairs on the back of my neck stood. I felt his fingertips land at the base of my neck, the heat of his touch filtering through the thin fabric of my shirt.

"Fiona," he said, his voice a raspy whisper.

His fingertips trailed down my spine. I felt each one like the lick of a flame on my skin.

"Hi," I whispered.

He leaned down, stepping closer to me. I felt the thick, hard length of his arousal press against me, nestling against my bottom. My pussy clenched, and I knew my panties were soaked.

"We have to hurry," I whispered.

"I need you."

The next moments were a blur. He took me by the hand and led me down the hallway into his office. I didn't even think about how risky it was that we walked down the hallway together. It wasn't far, but still.

The time burned like a flame racing down the wick on a stick of dynamite. We were in his office, and he was yanking my skirt up and bending me over his desk. His fingers delved between my thighs as he shoved my panties out of the way. I cried out.

"Fuck me, Fiona," he growled against my skin before he nipped lightly at the back of my neck.

My senses were attuned to everything. Hearing his zipper slide down was like a match striking over dry flint. When he dragged his cock through my slippery wet folds, I cried out, his name a plea as he notched his thick crown at my entrance.

He filled me in a single deep thrust, and I came almost instantly. My orgasm shook me to my very core.

He held still as I rippled around him before withdrawing and sinking in once more. I felt the heat of his release fill me as he shuddered behind me. His fingertips pressed deep into my skin where he held me by the hips.

I had never, *ever* come that fast in my life. But then, our foreplay started when I received his text earlier tonight. My body had been waiting for this moment, waiting to feel him joined with me. The sense of completion was more than physical. I felt it down to my bones, my heart setting a rapid drumbeat of undiluted emotion. The feeling was so profound that I almost didn't recognize myself.

My mind flickered back online as sensation spun through me in little eddies, a tide rushing out. My body felt like the air after a storm where it was cool and rinsed clean. Everything was brighter and clearer.

Blake curled around me with his forehead pressed between my shoulder blades and one arm wrapped around my waist. Although the embrace was perhaps awkward, it felt exactly right.

A few minutes later, he withdrew, and I missed him instantly. He helped me tidy my clothes. We stood in front of his desk. While a part of me felt bashful, I felt completely at ease on another level. It was almost too much. I couldn't believe I felt this way with him. I had never expected this. *Ever.*

I swallowed and lifted my lashes to look up at him. He studied me quietly. Although I knew him in many ways, in others, I didn't, not at all. He lifted a hand to brush my hair away from my face.

"I missed you." His voice was low and gravelly. It felt as if he had reached into my chest to hold my heart in his hand.

"I missed you too."

Just then, the sound of footsteps reached us. Time slowed as my eyes locked onto the doorknob of his office as it turned.

I leaped back. Then the door was open, and his brother Kenan was walking in. "Hey, man, I was looking for you —" He came to a quick stop as he glanced back and forth between us.

FIONA

Oh my God, oh my God, oh my God, oh my God, oh my God.

That was what replayed at double speed in my thoughts the following morning. That was all I could think when Kenan walked into Blake's office.

Blake had played it off and made a comment about chatting with me and David about some menu changes. Of course, that wasn't something we did. David didn't really check with Blake about menu things. Except for the weekly tastings, Blake was hands-off as far as the restaurant went.

I hadn't missed the speculation in Kenan's eyes when he looked at us. I knew my cheeks were deeply flushed. Just now, as I looked up at myself in the mirror, I blushed all over again.

"Mom!" Lia's voice reached me.

"Be right there!" I called.

I swiftly brushed my hair back into a tight ponytail. I might be having crazy-hot, filthy, intimate sex with one of the owners of the place where I worked and trying to keep it a secret from everyone, but for crying out loud, my hair would be tidy.

I hurried out of the bathroom and into the kitchen. Lia stood at the sink, looking up at my mother. "But I want pancakes," she pressed.

My mother arched a brow. "It's a school day. Cereal."

I wasn't about to dispute that point. Mornings were rushed enough as it was.

Lia turned and looked at me. "Mom, can I have pancakes?"

"Definitely not," I said.

Her dark brown eyes narrowed. "But I want pancakes."

"It's a school day. It's just like Gigi said. Cereal on school days. Is this why you were calling me?"

Lia let out a beleaguered sigh. "Yes."

"Sorry, but no pancakes."

Because she was a fairly good-natured kid,

after one more huff for good measure, she chose her favorite cereal. We didn't let her have "sugar" cereal, as she called it.

"Do you have your lunch money?" I asked.

Mornings were a well-oiled machine of rush. I sometimes wondered if anybody who had children got away from having insanely busy mornings. I just didn't know how anyone managed it without the madness.

By the time I pulled up to the drop-off line at school, I felt nearly breathless. The most relaxed part of my morning so far was the actual drive. During the drive, Lia peppered me with questions about dinosaurs. Needless to say, I was *not* an expert on dinosaurs.

When it got to be our turn, Lia unbuckled her seat belt and reached for her backpack on the floor between her feet. She smiled up at me. "Love you, Mom."

She blew a smacking kiss in my direction. I caught it with my hand, tossing it back to her in the air. "Love you too. Have a good day."

She scrambled out of the car and was gone in a flash. As I drove away, I smiled to myself, remembering when she'd started kindergarten and how nervous I was to get the drop-off line wrong. There were rules. So-cial media made that clear. Not that I had much time for social media, but I'd heard about people getting schooled for taking too much time.

Time was something I didn't have, so I never wasted it. I returned to the apartment, leaving the car for my mom. I planned to hurry upstairs and drop the keys off without dallying. I knew if I was around my mother for too long without the distraction of my daughter, she would pick up that I was unsettled inside. I wasn't ready for her questions because I was afraid I would end up blurting out the truth.

I'd already disappointed my mother enough in this lifetime. I didn't need to make things worse. I had just turned the car off when I felt my phone vibrate in my purse. It was sitting against the console on the other side so the whole console vibrated with the sensation. I slipped it out, and my stomach dropped. It was a text from that very number. I had labeled the contact *Go to hell*.

Hi, Fiona. This is your friendly reminder that you need to shut up. We know where you are and we know you work for the family that owns Fireweed Industries. If necessary, we know where to turn.

Dread coated the insides of my stomach, and I swallowed through the sting of nausea welling in my throat. I tapped the side of my phone to close out the screen and put it back in my purse. I wanted to jump out of my skin and run away from my life. I didn't know how to solve this.

I had a meeting at work, but I'd go tell Mike at the police station as soon as I could. There. I could at least do that.

This worry took my mind off Blake. I couldn't even think about anything other than this spinning concern.

I got through the weekly staff meeting at work. I was distracted, but I managed to offer some feedback about menu items when David was checking in on the flow of planning with the line cooks. As the group dispersed in the break room, David lingered. He was busy jotting notes in a notebook he always carried.

I slipped into the bathroom and checked the time to see that I had a full hour before I needed to be back for my shift. That would give me plenty of time to walk down to the police station. When I came back out, Kenan happened to be in there. Like Blake and the rest of the Cannon brothers I'd met, Kenan was handsome. Tall and well-built, he had brown hair and blue eyes. He had a hand resting on the back of one of the chairs by the round table in the corner, gesturing with the other as he talked with David.

As soon as I took a step, they both glanced over. I felt Kenan's gaze on me like an unwelcome blast. I didn't sense any judgment there, but I definitely felt his curiosity. It wasn't as if I needed a reminder that what I was doing with Blake was stupid, but the anxiety churning in my stomach reminded me just how foolish it was.

"Fiona, do you have a minute?" David called over.

I swallowed, willing the nervous feeling inside to dissipate as I approached the table. "Yes?"

"Any other changes you want to make for the special menus coming up?" he asked.

"I think everything sounds great."

Kenan glanced back and forth between us. "David, you're handling this adjustment better than I expected." His voice contained a hint of laughter.

David sort of glowered at him. "I told you I was ready to shift to just management. I can't tell you how grateful I am that Fiona handles the kitchen these days. My knees appreciate it, even if I miss the pace sometimes."

Kenan shifted to look at me. "It seems like it's working out well."

"It is. I'm really happy to be here." I took a quick breath. "If you don't mind, I have an errand to take care of before my shift."

I was relieved when David stood from the table. "See you when you're back. Kenan, come with me. I want to chat with Blake about his production schedule."

"Are you taking that over?" Kenan sounded genuinely surprised.

"Hell, no," David retorted as I walked toward my locker to get my purse out. "I want to get up to speed on any seasonal options that may be coming up so we can incorporate them into our specials." His voice faded as they disappeared down the hallway.

Moments later, I was walking down the sidewalk when a new thought struck me. *What if Kenan commented to David about finding me in Blake's office late at night?*

"Oh my God!" I shout-whispered under my breath.

Knowing there was absolutely nothing I could do other than panic, I kept walking toward the police station. A few minutes later, Mike was reading the text on my phone. "I don't like this," he said, almost as if he were talking to himself.

"I don't like it, either," I chimed in.

He lifted his gaze to mine, cracking a quick grin although his eyes were worried. "I'm going to photograph this and forward it to myself."

"Sure, go ahead."

"Don't delete it. We may need it if we can sort out who this is," he added.

"Did you have any luck when you reached out to the police in Seattle?"

"As soon as I mentioned the name of your ex, they put me in touch with their drug unit. For what it's worth, according to them, your ex was trying to untangle himself from the business, if you will." Mike grimaced when he said that. "They said he never got into dealing the heavy stuff. He stuck to prescription stimulants. Unfortunately, those are popular among high school and college kids. I'm sorry for what happened to him."

"Thank you," I said softly. My heart twinged with pain. "He was a good man. He really was. To this day, I know it surprised him how things turned out. I just wish..."

My words trailed off because I didn't even know what to say. I wished Johnny hadn't felt like he needed to find a way to help his family when he was in high school. I wished he had wised up to the risks of the path he started walking long before it was too late. And I *definitely* wished he had never accidentally mixed the wrong drugs.

"I'm only telling you this because they gave me permission to do so." Mike's voice broke through my trail of regrets. "Are you aware that your ex's death is still considered unexplained?"

At first, the meaning behind Mike's words didn't register. "Johnny died of an overdose. It was an accident," I said slowly.

Mike cocked his head to the side. "The detective told me there's some suspicion Johnny's drink was purposely spiked at the bar. The detective explained he wasn't known to use anything other than marijuana. If that happened, that could mean murder or manslaughter charges."

My mouth fell open as I stared at Mike. My pulse began to race at an unsteady pace. "I'm sorry, what?" I sputtered. My brain felt like it had tripped and stumbled. This didn't make sense.

The police chief nodded. "It's not unusual. From what I understand from the detective, your ex was an anomaly. Many dealers avoid using the heavy stuff, but most of them eventually begin dealing because it can be more profitable. From what the detective shared, Johnny had a well-established network, and people wanted to take advantage of that. He would be a mark. They gave me permission to tell you because they would like to interview you. Between these contacts to you and their suspicions, it's possible you may have information that can help them."

"Oh my God," I breathed.

"I thought this might be a shock to you. With you getting this follow-up text, I don't think we can sit on this. If you're willing to talk, we can schedule a time, and I'll be with you during the interview. The team from Seattle will be on a video call."

I was still reeling. I took an unsteady breath. "I don't know how I could help or what I might know. Johnny kept me mostly in the dark about this. I think he did that to protect me, but still."

Mike nodded. "You never know what you might know. They would have questions that might guide us."

I blinked and mentally gathered myself. "I'm certainly willing to talk with them. Of course, I want to help." I glanced at my watch. "I have to get to work soon."

"We need to schedule it with the detective who's handling the case, so I wouldn't worry about it happening today. What's your work schedule?"

Before I left, Mike assured me he would text me with some options for the interview once he heard back from the police in Seattle.

I left the police station with my mind spinning with yet another thing to worry about. As hurt as I had been by Johnny's choices and the destruction they brought into our lives, I had loved him. He had been good to me before everything skidded sideways. He had broken my heart, not because he hurt me, but because what he did wasn't safe for our daughter and for us. And now, to think perhaps he'd been targeted?

It was a shock wave. I'd fought my way through my grief. I didn't even know what to do with this.

Chapter Thirty-Three

BLAKE

Several days later

I didn't know what had happened, but I felt the distance Fiona put between us. When we passed by each other at work with nothing more than a glancing interaction, her gaze was carefully polite and her mouth was tight at the corners. I wanted to beat down the doors of her guard and remind her of what we had. I knew if I could get her alone, if I could get her bare naked and tangled up with me, she wouldn't be able to ignore the intimacy twining like two vines between us, getting stronger and stronger.

I had promised McKenna I would go to Willow Brook for the opening, and Wyatt and Griffin were going to be there. The event had gone from optional to my sister throwing me a look and insisting I not let her down. Our mother was going, and she *loved* when all her children were in one place.

With the recent discovery of her grand-son, my nephew, the son of our oldest brother who'd died in college and none of us had known about until recently, my mother's wish for us all to be close had grown more palpable.

Jake was gone, and the rest of us tried to make up for it. In all honesty, it mattered to me too. It's just I wanted to see Fiona. But this event yanked that opportunity out of my hands, at least for this weekend.

Missing Fiona, I flew to Willow Brook. Our half-brother, Chase, met us at the air-port. The whole story around Chase was its own little drama. Our father had a summer fling with Chase's mother before he met ours. So technically, Chase was our oldest brother. It was more of a drama for Chase than the rest of us. We got a bonus brother, and he got a whole family.

McKenna smiled up at him as she stepped back after giving Chase an enthusiastic hug. "You didn't have to come pick us up." She glanced over her shoulder.

"We're not all going to fit in one car," Kenan offered with a chuckle.

"I'm the other ride!" a female voice called.

McKenna beamed as she spun around to see Tiffany, Chase's sister, approaching. Tiffany was our bonus sister. McKenna was thrilled.

After exchanging hugs, we all piled into vehicles and headed out to Fireweed Industries' newly renovated location. Although I had grown up in a house full of siblings, many of those years had been fraught with tension, unfortunately. Between our father passing away when we were younger and our grandfather being an abusive asshole, it hadn't been great.

These days, even though we were all adults, it often felt like we were a pile of puppies, gamboling around each other with the old tension eased. Several hours later, the official event had come and gone, and we were all relaxing back at our cousin's house.

Archer was sitting beside me and glanced over with a grin. "So how are things with production at the brewery and winery?"

"Very good."

"What's the schedule for the winery and brewery here?" he asked.

Archer's wife, Phoebe, leaned around him, her brows arching up as she glanced over expectantly. "I'm dying to know. I'm really impatient."

I chuckled. "That's good to hear. I hope the rest of the town is impatient. Honestly, it slipped off my radar. I'll follow up with David. He's the one who manages the restaurant and retail location in Fireweed Harbor."

"I know he's the chef at the restaurant, but does he manage the whole retail end of things there?" Archer prompted.

Kenan sat down beside me, chiming in, "He always has. There's a lot to deal with in production and distribution. Blake's got his hands full."

"No kidding," I agreed. "It's incredibly helpful to have David run that whole end of things. I just help with the tastings."

"And he's still the chef?" Phoebe prompted.

"We hired a new one. This way, David has more time to focus on management," I said.

Archer's eyes went wide. "David is kind of a control —"

"A control freak," McKenna piped up as she plunked down in a chair nearby.

Kenan chuckled. "That's one way to put

it. He seems happy with Fiona. She's the new chef. It's been a seamless transition. He's even giving her some control as far as the menu and specials."

"Next time we come to town, we'll have to make sure to eat there," Phoebe commented.

"Don't you always?" McKenna teased lightly.

"We do." Archer winked. "So what is the scoop on the winery and brewery here? Rumors are popping up in town."

"I'll check with David. He intended to help plan everything here. We've got the location already. We might need some help locally." I glanced between Phoebe and Archer, adding, "If you know anyone who might want to help on that end, slide me their name. I'll make sure to put them on David's radar."

"Absolutely," Archer replied.

Conversation moved along, and the group began to disperse. Kenan and I were staying above the garage at Archer and Phoebe's home. There were two bedrooms up there, so it worked out well. When we walked over, his eyes slid to mine. "So what's going on with you and Fiona?"

Fuck. I was tempted to lie, but Kenan and

I were close. I knew he would know I was lying. "I promised her I would keep it quiet."

There. I wasn't admitting anything, not explicitly. Fuck.

"Well, I want you to keep that promise. But I'll say this, it's obvious you have a thing for her."

"Is it?" I prompted, trying to sound casual.

Kenan rolled his eyes before he began walking up the stairs that led to the small guest area above the garage. As he held the door at the top, he added, "Completely obvious. Maybe not to anyone who doesn't know you well, but when she's around, you're tense. You can't keep your eyes off her."

We walked inside together, and I let out a deep sigh. "Is it that obvious?"

Kenan kicked off his shoes and turned to face me fully. "Yes. I didn't think you were this careless."

I opened my mouth to protest before snapping it shut. I knew better, and I knew he had a point.

"It's going to come back to bite her, not you," he pointed out.

I shifted my shoulders, attempting to relieve the tension building there. "What if she really means something to me?"

Kenan's brows hitched up as he cocked his head to the side, studying me for a few beats. "If she really means something to you, I'd say be smart about it. Do you love her?"

Chapter Thirty-Four

FIONA

The following weekend

I reread Blake's text. *I really want to see you. It's been too long.*

I took a quick breath, staring down at my phone screen. I hadn't scrambled up the nerve to reply yet. I knew I had to end this reckless, insanely foolish fling with Blake. I never should've even let it begin.

I let out a sigh. I had done my interview with the police in Seattle and was profoundly grateful Mike had been with me. I had to tell my mother that Johnny might've been murdered by a spiked drink, all because people who worked with him knew he took stimulants. The drug test they did after he died showed cocaine and heroin in his system. The combination was fatal for him.

I could only hope they were going to make an arrest soon. They told me I'd given them some helpful information, which puzzled me. They sure had a lot of questions about our high school friends. Contemplating what that might mean made me feel a little sick.

The main suspect was one of Johnny's good friends from high school, Hank. They suspected he was the person texting me and using a different name. I thought we had actually been friends once upon a time. Mike reminded me afterward that desperate people often make bad decisions.

I finally lifted my phone again to reply to Blake's text.

Me: *I'm sorry, but I can't see you again. I'm sorry for everything.*

I returned my phone to my purse in my locker and dove into work. Blessedly, it was really busy. It felt as if my body was tuned solely to Blake. I sensed his presence every time he passed by the doorway into the kitchen. Aside from that, I was too busy to think about anything other than work.

Tonight was my late night. I went through my usual routines. Trepidation slipped through me as I walked down the hallway to the storage area. I hoped Blake didn't know my schedule.

I let out a sigh of relief when I pushed through the swinging doors into the front area again. Blake hadn't appeared, so maybe he'd accepted my response. As much as I missed him and as much as I wanted to see him, I didn't want to put his family in danger. As it was, they were at risk of being black-mailed. All because of me. I hoped he understood it was my reputation on the line, not his. That alone was reason enough for me to break things off.

A solid hour after I finished lining everything out for the morning, I went into the staff bathroom off the break room. I removed my hairnet and tossed it in the trash. After washing my hands and splashing water on my face, I stared in the mirror as I dabbed my face dry with one of the clean dish towels we kept in here.

I took a shaky breath and let it out with a sigh. A corner of my heart, soft and vulnerable, had fallen for Blake. Even though we hadn't spent much time together, I felt so good when I was with him. I felt safe and protected, a feeling I craved on a bone-deep level.

I couldn't just stand in the bathroom forever. I finished drying my face, took a deep breath, and slipped quietly out of the bathroom. Just as I shrugged into my jacket and closed my locker, footsteps entered the break room.

I knew without even looking that it was Blake. Instantly, my pulse skyrocketed. I took a slow, quiet breath and turned. He stopped a few feet away from me, his eyes searching mine.

"Can we talk? Please."

"Blake..." I began before pausing, trying and failing to gather my thoughts.

I didn't feel like I needed to explain. My role here in relation to his put me on shaky ground if we stayed involved. More than that, I absolutely did *not* want to talk with him about the situation with Johnny. That would mean being honest that whoever had hurt Johnny somehow knew my connection to the Cannon family and the potential mess that could create.

Blake took another step closer. "Just come to my office for a few minutes. At least, give me that," he pressed.

I nodded before I could think to stop myself. He held my eyes for a long moment before nodding. "I'll be there in five minutes. Meet me there."

Chapter Thirty-Five

BLAKE

Do you love her?

Kenan's question had feathered through my thoughts again and again and again since he'd asked it. I hadn't answered him. But I knew the answer.

I told Fiona to meet me in my office in five minutes. Less than a minute had passed since I walked in here. Anticipation thrummed through my body in a subtle vibration.

I stood from my chair and paced back and forth in front of my desk. I craved her on a visceral level. I needed her. Yet it was far more than a physical need and craving. My emotions were twined within it.

I didn't know how it was possible, but I'd

fallen in love with Fiona. I hadn't even had a full night with her, not one, not yet. Yet I understood her. Her deep loyalty for her daughter, her innate kindness, her quiet strength, and her fierce passion. Witnessing her when her guard fell felt like a gift, only for me. And even then, I knew she gave that gift reluctantly.

After what felt like far longer than five minutes, I heard the sound of the doorknob turning. I stopped pacing, turning to face Fiona when she padded into my office.

Her cheeks were flushed, and her eyes worried with a tiny furrow between her brows as she looked up at me. She'd taken off her coat. I presumed that if anybody happened to come into this office, it would seem strange she was ready to leave.

So as to prevent a repeat of when Kenan interrupted us, I stepped around her and locked the door. She practically leaped back away from me, creating distance between us.

When I faced her again, she began speaking immediately, her words tumbling out in a rush. "Blake, what do I need to explain? I think you already know this"—she gestured back and forth between us—"arrangement is a potential disaster for me. I need this job. Having the people I work with respect me is important to me personally. There's no risk for you, none at all. After Kenan came in the other night, I realized I had to stop this."

Her hands fell, and she laced her fingers tightly together. I stepped closer, reaching for her and sliding my hand down her forearm. Her hands fell apart, and I reached for both of them. They were cold and clammy.

"I understand," I said honestly. I didn't want what she said to be true, but I knew it. "I'd like to ask for one thing."

She looked up at me. At the sheen of tears visible in her eyes, my heart felt as if it cracked open, painfully.

"I want one night with you, just one whole night."

Her throat worked with her swallow, and the sound of her breath drawing in was loud in the quiet office. "Blake, what good would one night do for us?"

I released one of her hands, stepping closer and lifting my hand to trail my knuckles along the side of her cheek. "Maybe this is crazy, but I know it's not just sex, not for me. If I have to let you go, I want a night to remember."

She stared at me, starting to shake her head. I took another step, sliding my hand into her hair and wrapping my other arm around her waist to bring her flush against my body. I could feel the subtle tremors racing through her as she tried to hold back her tears. My own eyes stung from the emotion welling inside.

I let my head fall to rest beside hers as I breathed her in. We remained like that for I don't know how many minutes before I could feel her take a long, steadying breath. She lifted her head, leaning back slightly as she looked up at me.

My heartbeat was an echoing drumroll, pounding a crescendo of emotion, of my need, of my love for this woman who had somehow stolen my heart without even trying. We were still nothing more than a secret, yet that was how deeply and swiftly I had fallen.

"I understand," she whispered. "But even if I wanted to give you that night, it's not practical."

We stared at each other. The words *I love you* were clamoring to come out. But my own guardedness, my own lack of faith in the universe, held them back.

"Good night," she whispered as she stepped out of my embrace.

I heard myself replying in kind, my voice

low and husky. I watched as she disappeared out of my office, the snick of the door clicking shut behind her barely breaking through my awareness.

I stood there, bereft and with a sense of desolation gusting through me. I wanted to chase her down the hallway and demand anything more, something. But I had to let her go.

Chapter Thirty-Six

FIONA

"When?" I asked.

My mother didn't even glance over while she stirred oatmeal on the stove before turning off the flame underneath the small pot. "This Friday. You already signed the permission form. I told you I was going as a chaperone. Lia would be devastated if we canceled."

When she looked my way, her brows hitched up in question, a look of genuine confusion crossing her face. I had honestly forgotten this. I had no doubt I had signed the permission form and that Lia and my mother had talked to me about this. As usual, I was running on fumes just to keep up with life. Lately, I'd been more preoccupied. My heart was still achy and sore from breaking things off with Blake, work was incredibly busy, and the anxiety and fear related to the startling news about Johnny was bouncing around my thoughts every day.

I gave her a rueful smile as I shrugged. "I'm sure I signed the form. I wasn't even proposing that you cancel. It just slipped off my radar. When do you leave?"

"We take the ferry down there tomorrow. It's just one night. We're touring downtown Juneau, then attending a kids' theater production in the evening. You know how much Lia loves the theater. She's beside herself."

As if on cue, my daughter came skipping out. She spun in a circle when she stopped beside me, swinging her arms lightly. "Can you help me pack my bag? It's just for one night."

When you were a single mom, the idea of your child being gone for a whole night was both terrifying and thrilling. Of course, I couldn't even say I was truly a single parent these days. After Johnny and I broke up when Lia was four, it had just been me for a full year.

My mom would help whenever she could, but life felt like a scramble, the kind where I was almost always off balance and stumbling back to my feet again and again. After my father died, which had been completely devastating, my mom had proposed us living together. I had wanted her with us. She was grieving, and she adored Lia. It was the best thing for all of us. Even though I had my mother for help, money was constantly tight. It still was. I figured it always would be.

A night to myself seemed like a luxury. My belly spun with anxiety. Lia would be fine. She would be with my mother the entire time.

I internally cringed when I realized this opened a doorway I had considered firmly closed. I could have that one night with Blake. *Just one night*. No one would ever have to know.

I hastily helped my daughter pack the morning they were leaving. I waved as she and my mother stood by the deck railing on the ferry. There was a brisk, salty breeze blowing. "Love you!" I called.

Lia blew me a kiss and hurried to look over the railing facing the ocean. My mother laughed as she waved and turned to follow my daughter.

Emotion welled in my chest. My little girl was getting bigger every day. She was having adventures and learning new things. She loved living in Fireweed Harbor. She said it made her feel special because Alaska was special. She had already adopted the expression of calling the rest of the United States the Lower 48.

I breathed through the tightness in my chest. My heart filled with joy, and the bittersweet sense that time was slipping through my fingers as my daughter grew up.

A few minutes later, I sat in my car, staring at my phone. It had been a full week, and Blake had kept his distance. I was acutely aware of whenever he was nearby when I was at work, but I kept telling myself that would fade eventually. Maybe my heart would sting a little every time I saw him, and perhaps I would wonder whatever could've happened for us, but I would have a job, and my life would be stable.

I jumped in my seat when my cell phone vibrated in my hand. I stared at the number. It was that same guy. A sick feeling rose inside, and my stomach tightened uncomfortably.

Not a smart move to notify the police. Don't forget I can ruin your life. I can make things very awkward for you. The Cannon family has deep pockets. All you need to do is stay quiet. For Johnny.

My hands were shaking, the phone vibrating from my anxiety. I blinked away the tears welling. I thought it had been enough to lose Johnny and to lose the trust and faith I had in him before that. And now, this. It felt like someone was reaching through space and time to take me back to the very life I had tried to leave behind.

With a hard mental shake, I forwarded the text to the police chief. Then I called him.

"Fiona," Mike said as soon as he picked up.

"Hi, I just forwarded you a text. Obviously, that's stressful, but I was also wondering if you had any updates from the police in Seattle."

I heard him make a rustling sound. "Ah, that text just came through." He was quiet for a few seconds. "I know this is troubling, but keep in mind they've already made these threats. This is nothing new. I will send this to the police in Seattle. As for an update, I actually just heard from them this morning. I was planning to call you, but I hadn't had a chance yet."

"Oh, what's the update?"

"They are moving forward, and it looks like they've gathered enough evidence to make an arrest. The bar where your ex had that drink keeps all of their security footage, and they turned it over to the police. Hank was working behind the bar that night, and the footage shows him adding something to Johnny's drink. They're planning to interview him, but they also plan to arrest him. I'm not sure what the charges will be, but I'll definitely keep you posted. In the meantime, if they give me the go-ahead, I'd like to notify Rhys Cannon about this."

I couldn't hold back my gasp of dismay. "Is that really necessary?

"Fiona," he began, his tone calm and soothing. "I understand that you prefer the Cannon family isn't aware of this, but if anyone reaches out to them, it's best they know what's going on. I won't talk to them until the police in Seattle gives me the okay."

"Okay," I said, my voice sounding as small as I felt.

I knew what Mike said made sense. I wanted this situation to be over and for no one to have to know that I might have put the Cannon family at risk in any way. It felt as if the tiny island of stability I had found was about to be kicked out from under my feet.

After I finished my call with the police chief, I stared at my phone screen again. The unsettled feeling inside tipped me over the edge. I needed an escape. I craved feeling safe and protected. The way I did with Blake.

Me: *You said you wanted one night. What about tonight?*

My heart pounded madly in my chest, and my breath was short. The simple idea that I might be able to sleep beside Blake set my body to life, like air breathed into banked embers and sending sparks leaping into the air.

His reply came only a moment later.

Blake: *Yes. Come to my place. 8 p.m.*

BLAKE

My eyes swung to the clock on the wall in the kitchen. It was 8:02 p.m. I wondered if Fiona had changed her mind.

Or I'm fucking crazy because I'm obsessing about two minutes.

This was what happened when you wanted someone with every fiber of your being.

My life was now divided into two delineated times. Before Fiona. After Fiona.

Before Fiona, I'd have scoffed at the idea of falling for someone in the aftermath of only a few encounters. I'd have chalked it up to pure lust. Even though I kept trying to talk my heart out of it, I *knew* her.

I had stumbled into a back channel of information about Fiona when I stopped by my mother's house several days prior, only to find her in the kitchen having coffee with the woman who cleaned her house. That itself was nothing unusual. Except that woman was Fiona's mother. Natalie was singing Fiona's praises, talking about how much she'd given up to raise her daughter on her own after her ex passed away. How she'd been such a good student in high school but had to make some sacrifices.

It wasn't so much the details rather than the way Fiona carried herself. I knew why she worried about how people would perceive her if anyone found out about us. She was honorable and honest and caring. Gossip could be brutal. None of this started because Fiona thought she could get something. That was why she fought against it.

My senses were so finely attuned that I heard the sound of tires on gravel as soon as a vehicle turned onto my driveway. I walked swiftly to the front entrance, peering out the windows flanking the doorway. This was what I'd been reduced to, impatiently waiting for the woman I loved by the door.

My pulse kicked up a notch when I recognized her car. I was out the door and down the steps before she even closed her car door.

Fiona stopped a few feet away, staring at me in the light cast from the porch. "Hi," she said, her tone quiet.

"Hi."

We studied each other before she added, "Just one night."

I nodded as I reached for her hand. Once we were inside the house, I looked down. "Are you hungry?"

She shook her head.

"Good. I'd make you dinner, but that's not what I want right now." I pulled her close.

Her lashes lifted, and her eyes held mine. She leaned forward, pressing her lips into the divot at the base of my throat. Her kiss felt like a drop of hot honey landing on my skin, the sweet touch setting me on fire.

Her hair was up in a ponytail, high on her head, and pulled back tightly. I hooked a finger under the elastic. I didn't even have to speak, and she knew my question. At her nod, I slid the elastic free, watching her hair tumble loose.

In another second, we were kissing, and I forgot everything else.

Hours later, Fiona was asleep. She'd curled up against me with her chin tucked into the curve of my shoulder. My arm was wrapped around her with my palm resting in the dip of her waist. We had fallen asleep together.

I had wanted her with such ferocity, the force nearly leveled me, physically and emotionally. Yet it was *this*, this quiet time in the darkness, that I had wanted. I knew one night would never be enough. For now, it was all she had promised me. I would savor every second of it.

I shifted slightly, glancing down. Her face relaxed in sleep, the lines of tension smoothed away. Her lips parted just barely, and I could feel the steady gusts of her breath landing on my skin. My head fell back against the pillows. My heart almost ached. I was shocked at the depth of emotion Fiona brought to the surface for me.

Tonight, I had initially been driven by lust, passion, and untrammeled desire. But I had felt maybe fear, a depth of anxiety in Fiona that worried me and brought a sense of protectiveness roaring to the surface. It was as if she needed more than just us, as if she was seeking comfort in me, in the fire that burned between us.

I would have to keep my questions to myself. I sensed she would brush me off if I dared to ask.

I still had that niggling worry about the situation she had gone to the police about. But I had checked with the police chief weeks ago, and he had told me he was following up. I had faith he would. I would have to wait and hope for the best.

I shifted slightly, bringing Fiona a little closer as if I could imprint her on my body, a visceral memory to hold.

Chapter Thirty-Eight

FIONA

I was warm, so very warm. I savored the feeling. As my brain flickered out of sleep, I remembered I was with Blake.

Recollections spun in my thoughts of being wrapped in his arms, him filling me from behind, and then later as I sat astride him. Yet again when he tugged me into the shower and kissed me senseless against the tiled wall as hot water rained down around us.

And then, *finally* falling asleep beside him, feeling safe, protected, and utterly sated.

For just a moment, I let myself imagine we could have more than this. I let that wish go like a cloud drifting away. Because that wasn't my life. To think I had once only worried about my reputation. Now, I had to worry about protecting his family somehow.

I knew they would all be horrified once they found out. Perhaps the judgment wouldn't be too harsh, and they would understand that I had nothing to do with it except for bad luck and falling in love with the wrong man. But they would certainly not want anyone in their family to be tangled up with me in any serious way. There was the wrong side of the tracks, and then there was my messy life.

I wanted to stay in this bed forever, with Blake's arm curled around me and his palm splayed at my waist with his fingers curving onto my bottom. I wanted to breathe him in, to absorb the scent of him into my very being so I could carry him with me. His scent was masculine and musky with an edge of crispness. Even now, I thought I could smell the ocean on him.

I took a slow breath and carefully slipped out of bed, hoping I wouldn't wake him.

No such luck. His eyes opened, meeting mine. It wasn't even dawn yet. Nothing more than slivers of light could be seen above the mountains outside his bedroom window. His silver-gray eyes matched the light itself.

"Do you have to go so early?" His voice was soft with velvety edges.

Emotion rushed through me. I felt tears wicking up from my throat into my eyes. I blinked them away. "I do."

He didn't say a word as he slipped out of bed. Within minutes, I was dressed and standing by the doorway. "Just last night?" he asked.

I nodded, not trusting myself to speak. He gave me a quick and fierce kiss before I left.

Restless and keyed up inside, I decided to stop at Spill the Beans Café. I knew when I got home that my apartment would feel empty, and I would feel at loose ends.

Despite the near complete distraction of Blake last night, I had texted my mom and Lia before I drove over to his place. With my daughter's bedtime at eight, it was convenient because no one would expect me to text later than that.

Now that I had closed the door on Blake, I knew if I went home too soon, I would start missing him. Silly though it was, I had somehow hoped that spending one night with him would make it easier to say good-bye. Instead, those cracks in my heart kept spreading wider. I doubted my choices on every level. I wished I had never, *ever* let that first kiss happen with him.

I dropped my car off at my apartment and set off on the short walk to the café. Having grown up in a city, I hadn't known how much I would love the sense of community here and enjoy the feeling of getting to know life in this small town.

I loved that our apartment was right in the heart of downtown Fireweed Harbor. I could even walk to the grocery store. I paused to look over at the harbor, my eyes landing on that bench where I had encountered Blake. My heart twisted sharply in my chest. I took a deep breath of the briny, crisp, and cool ocean air before turning away and hurrying to the café.

The scents of coffee and fresh baked goods assailed me when I entered. I glanced around, feeling my lips curl into a smile. When I approached the counter, only one person was in line ahead of me—an elderly woman I often saw when I came through here.

Phyllis was waiting on her, and she looked up with a quick smile as she gave the woman her change. The woman turned around, her sharp blue eyes studying me. "You must be

Fiona Thompson," she said, her weathered face cracking with a smile.

"I am," I said hesitantly.

Phyllis gestured me closer to the counter, offering, "Mimi, this is Fiona. Don't terrify her."

Mimi let out a sly laugh. "I don't terrify people."

Phyllis rolled her eyes. "Fiona, this is Mimi Smith. If you're wondering how she knew who you were, it's because she basically knows everyone."

Mimi waggled her brows, resting a hand on her hip. She was slender and tiny. I could imagine too much wind might blow her away. She brought her attention to me again. "I know who you are because you're the new chef at Fireweed Winery. I should've placed bets on whether or not you'd last."

"Mimi," Phyllis warned.

"What would you have bet?" I couldn't help but ask.

"I would've bet that you would've lasted, and you have. I have faith in David. Cranky though he can be, I didn't think he would hire someone who wouldn't last. Other people just assumed he wouldn't like anyone. I said if he didn't like anyone, he wouldn't hire them. Turns out, I was right. Consider this a belated welcome to Fireweed Harbor."

I let out a startled laugh. "Well, it's nice to meet you."

She cocked her head to the side, her sharp gaze studying me for another beat. "You as well. I'm sure I'll see you around town." She held her coffee cup aloft as her gaze swung to Phyllis. "Thank you again."

A gust of cool air swirled inside as Mimi left the café. When I glanced back at Phyllis, she shook her head and looked amused.

"What is it?" I asked.

"Mimi. She's a love, but she can be intimidating. She also knows everything. If you want to keep a secret, keep that in mind."

My conscious pricked, but I ignored it. Hopefully, my two biggest secrets, my past and my reckless fling with Blake, would remain secrets.

I shrugged. "I don't have much to hide. Here's hoping it stays that way."

Phyllis had started to get my coffee ready when the door opened again. When I glanced back, I saw Haven walking in.

Another woman was with her. Haven smiled when she stopped beside me. "Hey, Fiona." She gestured to the woman beside her. "This is Tessa. I'm getting some tea while she has coffee."

"That's what people do here," Phyllis interjected dryly.

"Sit with us," Haven said, nudging me lightly with her elbow.

I looked hesitantly at Tessa. "Are you —"

"Please, sit with us," Tessa interjected.

I didn't have many friends. Not that I didn't want them, but time wasn't something I had. I had learned to keep to myself after I had my daughter. I was out of sync with most of my peers and swimming fast just to stay afloat in the currents of life. I had promised myself Fireweed Harbor was a fresh start. Making friends here was on the list of goals I had. Nothing I'd ever written down, but I held that wish in my thoughts.

A few minutes later, we were sitting at a table in the corner. Haven lifted a hand to brush a few strawberry-blond curls out of her eyes. "So I hear nothing but great things about you at the winery."

Before I could respond, Tessa chimed in, "I love the menu updates and the new specials. I go to locals' night on the regular."

My cheeks flushed a little as I smiled between them. "Thank you. I was a little nervous with David having handled things for so long."

"David's great, but this is a good change for him. Is he being nice to you? I know he can be cranky," Haven said, her brow furrowing as she looked over at me.

"Honestly, David and I get along well. You just have to get used to him. I've learned he can come across as crabby, but he's very supportive of everyone. He's just not really a warm and fuzzy guy."

Tessa snorted. "No, he's not."

"You both seem to know him well," I observed.

"Aside from the fact that I'm dating Rhys, Fireweed Winery is a staple in town. My brother used to work there in high school as a bus boy."

"And David's my uncle," Tessa added.

"Oh!" I was surprised at that detail.

Tessa's lips curled with a smile. "David is private. If you grew up around here, you'd know I was his niece, but even then, he keeps to himself. He claims he doesn't want to get caught in the gossip machine. He's my father's brother—never had kids and dedicated his life to his job. I wish he would fully retire, but he tells me he's not even close to ready for that."

"I like David. I was nervous at first, but he's been really supportive," I added.

I took a sip from my coffee, glancing over when someone approached the table. McKenna stopped beside Haven's chair, resting her hand on Haven's shoulder and giving it an affectionate squeeze. "Good morning, ladies."

After exchanging greetings, she and Haven chatted briefly about some promotional project before McKenna turned her attention to me. "You know..." She paused, tapping her fingertip against her chin. "We could have Fiona give us the specials in advance and include the menu as part of our promotional materials. What do you think?"

I smiled politely. "I'm happy to help, as long as it's okay with David."

McKenna shrugged. "I need to clear it with him first. By the way, things seem to be going really well in the kitchen."

I was nervous, mostly because McKenna was Blake's sister. Ever since Kenan had walked into Blake's office that night, I worried he suspected something and might have talked to someone else in the family. I kept telling myself I was overreacting, but it didn't soothe me.

"Thank you," I said simply, masking my

anxiety with another swallow of coffee.

Tessa caught my eyes while Haven and McKenna continued chatting. "The Cannon family can be a lot."

Uncertain of what to say with McKenna standing right there, I simply shrugged. "I suppose so."

Just then, a frisson of awareness chased down my spine. I knew Blake had just entered the café. I tried to order my pulse to slow its pace, but it had none of it and went wild, like a horse let loose in the pasture, taking off at a mad dash.

Because my body was disobedient, I glanced over my shoulder to see him walking to the back of the line. As if he sensed my presence, he turned, and our eyes met. Instantly caught in the beam of his gaze, sparks spun in fiery pinwheels inside.

I forced myself to look away, relieved the café was busy, and McKenna was still talking to Haven.

"He's right over there," Haven said.

I almost groaned aloud when she gestured toward Blake. "Blake!" McKenna called over. When he looked her way, he simply arched a brow in question. "Come over here once you get your coffee. I have a question," she added.

Chapter Thirty-Nine

FIONA

I could barely breathe. I was terrified people would take one look at me and somehow know I had spent the night tangled up bare naked with Blake. I thought about Phyllis's comment about keeping secrets in this small town. Despite my near panic, I knew I had made the right decision when I told Blake we could only have the one night. I didn't dare to let myself fall any further for him. I was already in *way* too deep. As it was, I feared my heart would need to be stitched up after this.

I took a bite of my muffin, chewing madly, as if I could chew away my anxiety. No one seemed to notice that I was a hot mess with McKenna asking for my opinion on seasonal promotional menus. I managed to answer, if only because I loved to cook and had recipe ideas bouncing around in my brain all the time.

Blake arrived by our table, and I allowed myself nothing more than a quick glance at him. I squeaked out a greeting when he said, "Hello, Fiona."

I barely heard McKenna and Haven talking to him. "Well, you'll have to ask David," Blake pointed out.

"He'll say yes," Tessa chimed in.

"I'm sure Fiona will have some ideas. The changes you've made to the menu are great," Blake added. I felt the burn of his gaze, almost as if it were flames on my skin.

I simply nodded. I would have to get used to this, to learn to live with how much I wanted him. I was relieved when he left and even more relieved when McKenna left with him. I didn't realize I'd been holding my breath until the door closed behind them, and I let it out in a quiet sigh.

A woman stopped by the table, asking Tessa something about the weather. Haven caught my eye, offering, "She's our local weather reporter."

"Oh." My conversational skills had dwindled in the presence of Blake and McKenna.

After the woman moved on, Tessa glanced at me with a teasing look in her eyes. "Blake totally has a thing for you."

I had just taken a sip of coffee and almost choked on it. Haven helpfully patted me on the back. After I composed myself, I looked over at Tessa. "No way."

"No way, what?" Haven prompted.

"There's no way Blake has a thing for me. Even if he did, it can't go anywhere."

"Why not?" Tessa asked.

"Um, he's sort of my boss," I pointed out.

Tessa shrugged, all unconcerned. "Not directly. Fireweed Industries is huge. Blake runs all the production and distribution. David is your boss."

"The Cannon family owns the restaurant," I said, thinking she had lost her damn mind.

Haven shrugged. "Fireweed Harbor is a small town. Blake's not your direct boss. It's not that I don't understand being a little anxious about it, but..." Her words trailed off as she cocked her head to the side. "Blake is a nice guy. I'm not saying you should do anything about it, but I stand by what Tessa said. He's got the hots for you."

When I arrived at work a short while later, I reminded myself it didn't matter what

Tessa or Haven thought. I had already set the boundary with Blake, and I needed it to stay that way. Of course, even my bossy thoughts couldn't overpower just how much I wanted things to be different.

What if it could work?

Chapter Forty

BLAKE

Walking into my brother's office, I asked, "What's up?"

Rhys had texted me, asking me to stop by his office. He'd said it was important. He wasn't one for drama, so if he said it was important, it was.

He held a finger up, saying into his phone, "I'll be sure to let you know. Thank you for calling."

I sat in the chair across from his desk when he ended his call. "What's going on with you and Fiona?"

His question took me off guard. I felt my mouth begin to drop open and snapped it shut. Not fast enough. He took a breath. "Ah, so something is going on?"

"I didn't say that," I countered. "And why are you even asking?"

"Because Kenan mentioned it. The only reason he mentioned it is because he just left my office. We have a situation, and it involves Fiona."

I was tempted to play it cool, but I sensed I knew what this might be about, so I waited.

"Did you know about this?" he prompted.

"It depends on what you mean. I do know that someone in her past contacted her about her ex. To my knowledge, it had nothing to do with us. She was worried, and I suggested she talk with the police here."

Rhys studied me. "It's more complicated than that now. They threatened her with blackmailing us."

"What?" Anger blazed through me. "She would've said something to me. Are you sure about this?"

"Absolutely. I just got off the phone with Mike from the police department here. Everything should be okay. According to him, the police in Seattle are arresting the guy they believe is making the threats. Mike wanted to alert me in case anybody in the family gets contacted."

I heard what my brother was saying, but

my thoughts were a jumble. I was shocked and hurt Fiona would hide this from me.

"With that out of the way, just how serious are you with Fiona?"

"We're not. She broke it off," I said curtly.

He studied me quietly, his gaze uncomfortably perceptive. "You know, you're not her direct boss, but it's not a good look for you to be fooling around with anyone who works for us."

"It's not like that," I ground out.

I was torn between hurt that Fiona hadn't kept me up to speed on the situation and a sense of worry and protectiveness for her.

"If it's not like that, then what is it like?" my brother pressed.

"Fuck." I leaned forward, resting my elbows on my knees as I ran my hands through my hair. Lifting my head, I repeated, "Fuck."

"Fiona doesn't strike me as the type to just have a fling with one of the owners of the place she works." Rhys's tone was deceptively calm, but I knew he was angry—not with her, with me.

"She's not." I let out a frustrated breath. "It's not a fling. She means a lot to me."

"So much that you didn't know about the situation?" His tone was pointed now.

"She told me we had to break it off," I

muttered. "And I promised her I would respect that even though it's not what I want."

Rhys nodded slowly. "Maybe you should at least talk to her about this. If Kenan noticed, I doubt he's the only one. I don't care about your reputation, but she doesn't deserve the blowback from this. If she really means a lot to you, maybe think about what you want to do about that."

"I love her," I burst out, startling myself.

Rhys's brows hitched up. "Maybe you should tell her. If this isn't just a fling, the gossip will blow over. You know how rumors are in this town. Even if none of us says a word, the likelihood that somebody knows something about you two is near one hundred percent."

Over the next few days, with Rhys's observation ringing in my mind, every time I saw Fiona at work, I was caught up in conflicted feelings. I understood his point about how she would face the consequences of any rumors and not me. I'd known that all along. Yet I had wanted her too much and ignored the potential pitfalls for her. I didn't like thinking I'd been selfish, but I had.

I skipped tracks from that train of thought to the stinging betrayal I felt that Fiona hadn't told me all that was going on.

It's not like she owes you anything, my better self pointed out. *What would you have done if she had told you?*

The protectiveness I felt for her was fierce.

I told myself over and over I wasn't going to push her again. I wasn't going to ask for more than she was willing to give. I would respect the boundaries she had set. I was learning what it meant to love someone. Before, my desperation for Fiona had ridden roughshod over my ability to think rationally about the situation and the potential consequences for her. Now, I would sacrifice for her because I loved her. I would let her go *because* I loved her.

It would hurt like fucking hell, but I would do it. We needed to have one last conversation, just one.

Late one evening when I knew she was closing, I sent her a text.

Me: *I'm going to be here late tonight. I'm hoping we can talk. I promise I'm not asking for anything more.*

After I set my phone down, impatience churned inside me, rising like a restless tide. I kept trying to brush away the betrayal I felt. I was deeply hurt. I suppose I realized that maybe Fiona didn't feel what I felt. Maybe it was all a mirage in my mind.

Even though I knew she was busy, I kept expecting her to respond to my text quickly. She didn't. It was a solid two hours before she replied.

Fiona: *OK. I'll stop by your office.*

I had to take a deep breath and talk myself down. I wasn't usually an irrational guy. But when it came to Fiona, reason and rational thought jumped out the window and fled into the darkness.

BLAKE

There was a light knock on my office door, so soft it was barely audible. My senses were on hyper-alert, so attuned to Fiona that when the air circulation system came on, the sound caused me to nearly jump out of my chair.

Maybe that was why I was so keyed up. Perhaps that was why I ended up overreacting.

I didn't realize I had stopped breathing when I opened the door until she prompted, "Blake?"

I sucked in a startled breath of air as I stepped back. "Come in." My voice was strained, sharp.

Fiona looked like she usually did—buttoned up and tidy. Her hair was pulled back tightly. Her cheeks were pink, and her eyes wide. She laced her fingers together in front of her waist. "You wanted to talk with me?"

I'd planned out what I meant to say. I would tell her that I understood why she ended things. I would tell her that I had let my emotions and need get the best of me. I would tell her it hurt me that she hadn't shared the full extent of what she was dealing with.

That wasn't how it went.

"Why didn't you tell me what was going on? I had to hear the whole story from Rhys. That this guy threatened to blackmail us to get you to do what he needed. I thought you trusted me."

Her nostrils flared, and her eyes narrowed. "This isn't about trust. I was trying to protect my life. I have a daughter. I did exactly what you said and talked to the police. I'm more sorry than you know."

After she stopped talking, she held my gaze for a moment. Without another word, she spun and reached for the door handle. I caught her by the elbow, dropping my hand when she turned back. "Fiona—"

She shook her head sharply. "It doesn't matter, Blake. All of this was a mistake. I'm sorry."

A second later, she was gone. I felt the aching beat of my heart almost painfully. I walked to my desk, resting my hands on it with my head hanging down as I tried to collect my thoughts. I couldn't think straight. I couldn't fix this. Fiona had every right to keep her distance from me and wish this had never happened. Yet that wasn't what I wanted. I wanted her. I wanted it to be okay. I wanted *us*. More than anything, I wanted to be the one she turned to when she needed someone.

Yet I wasn't.

Chapter Forty-Two

FIONA

Three weeks later

I was closing one evening. Notebook in hand, I began walking down the hallway toward the dry storage. My heart started beating faster, and I tried to tell my body to get a grip, to remember that it was over with Blake. Completely over.

Blessedly, the other thing that was over was the situation related to Johnny's death. They had arrested and charged his old friend with manslaughter and obstruction of justice. Apparently, he had done some things to interfere with the original investigation when Johnny died.

Johnny and his old friend had a falling out a few weeks before Johnny died because Johnny had been trying to end his involvement in the business. My heart felt broken all over again to realize Johnny had been trying to do what he could to extract himself from the mess he'd gotten tangled up in.

As painful as this news was, I could breathe a little easier now. No one would be threatening the life I was trying to build for my daughter.

I still didn't know how to ever tell our little girl what happened to her father. I knew I could try to keep it a secret, but eventually, she would find out. Because that was how things went. My mother suggested we plan to tell her when she was old enough to understand, but no sooner.

How old was old enough for someone to understand that their father had made some bad decisions? That he ended up dying because of those decisions? But that he had also been a good man who didn't know better when he was too young? Those questions tumbled around in my thoughts on repeat. I'd have to figure them out when the time came. Maybe I didn't know when old enough to understand was yet, but I was pretty sure it wasn't first grade.

I slipped quietly into the storage room.

At the sound of footsteps, my heart gave an achy beat. That was the messy thing about all of this. Even though I knew it was the best decision, I missed Blake terribly. A corner of my heart wished he would walk in and wrap his arms around me. I could breathe him in and lean into his strength.

I glanced over my shoulder to see him walking by the storage room. His eyes met mine from a distance. He kept walking.

It's for the best was my mantra. It had to be, even if it didn't feel good.

Ten minutes later, I was walking back toward the staff break room when Blake came out of the swinging doors leading into the bar area. He was laughing with Kenan, who walked at his side.

Blake lifted his head when my shoes squeaked on the floor as my stride stuttered. My heart clanged along in my chest. It was all I could do not to burst into tears when he walked by with nothing more than a polite smile. Kenan glanced sharply back and forth between us but didn't say anything.

I rushed into the staff bathroom, closing the door and leaning against it. I pressed my fist to my mouth to keep from sobbing aloud. My tears slid down my cheeks in silence.

———

I knocked on David's office door, praying he called me in quickly. My eyes darted to Blake's office door a little farther down the hall.

"Come in!" David called through the door.

Stepping inside, I closed it behind me, needing the physical boundary between myself and Blake's office. David smiled over at me from where he was seated at a small round table in the corner. "Fiona, have you met Quinn?" He gestured to a woman seated beside him. Kenan was sitting across from them.

"I don't believe I have," I replied as I walked across the office to stop beside the table.

The woman smiled up at me. "I'm Quinn Blackthorn. I'm one of the attorneys for Fireweed Industries. While we haven't formally met, I usually come to locals' night, so I've had some of your specials. Should I say chef's kiss? Or would that be cliché?" She teased lightly as her gaze slid to David.

David chuckled.

"We're thrilled with how Fiona is working out," Kenan chimed in.

"That we are," David replied with a firm nod.

"Nice to meet you, Quinn," I said with a quick smile. Glancing at David, I added, "I thought we were meeting now to go over the upcoming event?"

David looked puzzled before he shook his head. "Obviously, I forgot to put it on my calendar. Why don't you finish up for lunch in the kitchen, and we can meet after that? Will that work?"

"Of course. I don't have to pick up Lia until later because she has a field trip to the harbor this afternoon."

"Perfect," David replied.

"Good to see you both," I said, casting a quick smile at Kenan and Quinn.

My eyes landed on Kenan as I turned to leave. The look in his eyes was unmistakable. He was staring at Quinn as she said something to David. If it was possible for the air to actually spark with the heat of his gaze, it would've. As I walked down the hallway, I thought to myself maybe they would make a good couple.

My heart felt stung again. I hated missing Blake and wished I'd had enough sense never to kiss him.

Later that afternoon, I was finishing up

my meeting with David when my cell phone vibrated. I ignored it, but it persisted. Someone was calling me repeatedly. I finally glanced toward David. "I think I need to get that."

"Of course."

I slipped my phone out to see that it was the school calling. "Hello?"

"Fiona, this is Tessa."

"Oh, hi, Tessa," I said uncertainly.

"I was at the harbor doing a weather report, and Lia was there with her class. I'm calling because there's been an accident."

Moments later, I was running down the hallway, the sound of my shoes thumping on the floor with every step. My hands were shaking as I jumped in my car.

Lia had fallen off the docks. To add to my panic, there had been a sea lion in the water. The only other information I had was they'd gotten her out of the water and taken her to the hospital to be checked out.

I gripped the steering wheel tightly as I drove, not even caring if I was speeding. I skidded into the emergency room entrance moments later, my shoes squeaking as I came to a stop in front of the desk. "Hi!" My chest heaved from my panting.

A woman looked up. "Yes?"

"Fiona!" Turning, I saw Tessa hurrying down the hallway.

She glanced at the woman at the reception desk. "This is Lia's mom. Can she just come right to the room with me?"

"Of course."

In my panicked state, all I could imagine was that Lia was bloodied and on the verge of death. Instead, the sight of her with her feet swinging where she sat on the examination table wrapped in a blanket greeted me.

I burst into tears.

Chapter Forty-Three

BLAKE

I was handing money across the counter to pay for some coffee at Spill the Beans Café when Haven came through the back. "Hey, are you covering a shift today?" I asked.

"Just for an hour or two. Phyllis had an appointment to get blood work done. She should be back soon."

Just then, Phyllis appeared behind her. "I'm back now." She looked straight at me. "You should go to the hospital."

"Uh, why?"

"Because your girlfriend's daughter is there," she said calmly.

"What?" I practically barked at Phyllis.

"I saw them when I was leaving. She's okay, but they had a field trip after school to the harbor. I don't know the whole story, but from what I can gather, she got excited when she saw a sea lion and slipped and fell into the harbor."

I didn't say another word before I spun around, jogging out. Haven was behind me, calling, "Let me come with you!"

I turned to look at her, only then realizing that Phyllis had referred to Fiona as my girl-friend. "Hop in."

A minute later, I was speeding down the street to the hospital. "Are you okay?" Haven asked.

"No. I'm not," I said sharply.

"Phyllis said Fiona's daughter was okay."

"I know, but—" I cut myself off.

"I know," Haven said softly.

"You know what?" I stopped at the light before I turned onto the road leading to the hospital.

"About you and Fiona. Rhys told me. He told me I couldn't mention it to anyone."

"Of course, he told you," I muttered.

"He said he thinks you love her."

The light changed, and I turned, trying to ignore the clanging of my heart in my chest. "I do love her." Just saying the words out loud, my heart felt raw. "How the hell does Phyllis know anything about Fiona and me?"

Haven cast me a knowing look as I came to a jerking stop in the parking area outside the emergency room. "Phyllis usually knows more than I know about myself. I understand from Rhys that you two were trying to keep it quiet, but it's really hard to keep any secrets in Fireweed Harbor. You know that."

"Fuck," I muttered. "I just hope there's no gossip about Fiona."

Minutes later, I paced in the waiting area. I had texted Fiona, but no one let us back to see her and her daughter. Logically, I understood. We weren't technically family, but I was furious. I just wanted to ensure Lia was okay and that Fiona was okay.

"Hey, guys," Tessa said.

Spinning around, I barked, "Is Lia okay?"

Tessa stopped in front of us, studying me for a beat. "She'll be fine. She got scratched on the piling. They gave her a sedative so they could thoroughly clean it."

"She got scratched on a dock piling?"

Tessa nodded. "She's been a very good sport about it."

"Where is Fiona?" I demanded.

"She's waiting down there." Rosie appeared beside Tessa. They were both good friends of Haven's, and Rosie was a nurse here. "I'll take you down there, but you'd better be on your best behavior."

I rolled my eyes. "Of course."

As I contemplated how to talk to Fiona in front of all these people, Rosie did me a solid. When we came to the door of the room where Fiona waited, she stopped. "We'll wait out here."

I stepped into the room. Fiona stood by the windows with a balled-up tissue in her hands.

Her eyes were red from tears, and her cheeks were damp. I was standing in front of her in three strides. "Lia's okay?"

Fiona nodded and sniffled. I didn't even think. I simply wrapped her in my arms, a sense of relief washing through me when she didn't resist. She tucked her head into the side of my neck and took a deep, shuddering breath.

We stayed like that for several long moments. It felt as if we communicated without words.

I missed you. She's okay.

You're okay. We're okay. I missed you too.

"I don't want to keep us a secret," I spoke aloud, my words clear.

She lifted her head, peering up at me. "What?" Her voice was raspy from crying.

"I don't want to keep us secret. I understand why you were worried, but it'll be fine. It's not a huge scandal. I was hurt before because I thought maybe the way I felt wasn't how you felt."

Her eyes held mine. It felt as if she were holding her breath.

"I love you."

Her eyes widened, and she let out a startled breath. "You do?"

I brushed a loose lock of hair off her cheek. "I do. Even though I didn't understand it when I first found out, I know you were trying to protect my family."

A tear rolled down her cheek, and I brushed it away with my thumb.

"I love you too. I know it's not convenient, and—" she began.

"It doesn't matter. I'm not your boss. David is. Before you think people will judge you, those who do are assholes. And those who matter won't judge you."

Her eyes searched mine, and I could see the questions swirling. "Blake, we're so different. I can barely pay the bills, and I'm a single mom, and—"

"You're a single mother who has been taking care of her daughter and her mother on her own after a really difficult situation with her ex. I'm sorry about what happened to him. I know it must hurt to learn that. We're not as different as you think. My family didn't always have money. I understand what it means to have someone who has lots of money saying it's not a big deal to have lots of money. I'm just saying we're not the kind of family who looks down on people who work hard and make a life when circumstances don't break their way." I cupped her cheeks and bent low to bring my lips to hers. Straightening, I repeated, "I love you."

She took a shuddering breath. "I love you."

"Tell me about Lia. She's okay, right?"

"She is. She wasn't even crying." She let out a little laugh. "I just panicked. She's never gotten hurt, no more than a scraped knee, which is kind of amazing since she's a pretty active kid."

"When we were walking down, Rosie told me they were cleaning the scratches."

Fiona nodded. "The pilings have barnacles on them, so she got a nasty scrape on her leg. My mom should be here soon."

Just then, there was a soft knock on the door. "Fiona!" someone called before another voice demanded, "Let me in there to see her."

Fiona's mother walked in, her perceptive

gaze bouncing from me to Fiona. "I knew it," she announced.

Fiona jumped back, cheeks flushing pink. Her mother clucked. "No need to hide. I know this is your friend."

I bit the insides of my cheeks to keep from laughing. "How do you know?" Fiona countered.

"Honey, this is a small town, and I know you. I saw you two when he dropped you off with your car. All I had to do was see the way you looked at him." She glanced at me. "And the way you looked at her. If you hurt her, I will make your life a living hell. My daughter has already been through too much."

I held up both palms. "I love Fiona."

Chapter Forty-Four

FIONA

When Blake so openly declared his love in front of my mother, Rosie, the nurse I'd just met who'd told me earlier I was going to be her newest friend, Haven, Tessa, and David who appeared in the doorway at that moment, I thought my heart might burst. I also wanted to melt into the floor.

When I looked toward David, he must've sensed my worry because he winked. "Hard to keep a secret around here." His gaze swung to Blake. "I've known you since you were a little boy. I'm with her mom. You'd better not hurt her."

Hours later, Blake had driven us home, and my mom had followed with my car. Lia was thrilled with the events of the day. For her, it was an exciting story to share.

After Blake dropped us off, he graciously told me he'd see me the next day. Even though I was beyond relieved that our emotions were out in the open, I couldn't spend the night away from Lia, not tonight. When I went to check on Lia before turning off her bedroom light, just as I was about to stand from her bed, she commented, "I like Mr. Blake."

I stopped, sliding my hips back onto the bed. "I do too."

"He's your special friend," she pointed out, as if she were giving me permission.

A few minutes later, I was still marveling over her. When I shared what she said with my mother, my mother grinned. "She's the one who first made me wonder about you and Blake. She said you kept looking at him. She also said the air felt 'special'"—my mother emphasized with air quotes—"when he gave you a ride. It sure seems like Blake really loves you."

"But—"

My mother walked over to stand in front of me, placing both hands on my shoulders. "You are a good mother. Blake is a good man.

You're allowed to fall in love again. It will be okay."

Chapter Forty-Five

FIONA

Two days later

My heart felt like a bird caught in the cage of my ribs, fluttering about anxiously. I stood in front of Blake's house, trying and failing to steady my nerves. I lifted my hand to knock just as the door opened. His eyes caught mine instantly. It felt as if that bird flew skyward in my chest in a burst of joy and excitement.

Emotions stormed through me—joy, anticipation, anxiety, desire, and still a tinge of fear threading through all of it. The past two days had been busy with the weekly tasting at the winery, along with the usual madness. It felt as if the whole world of Fireweed Harbor knew about Blake and me. Apparently, I was terrible at keeping a secret and hiding my feelings.

For this moment, I didn't have to hide my feelings. I pressed my palm to my chest as if I needed to physically contain my heart. Tears were hot in my eyes, and I didn't even realize one rolled down my cheek until Blake stepped across the threshold and murmured, "Hey, no need to be upset."

I swallowed through the knot in my throat as I shook my head. "Those are happy tears." I sniffled.

He folded me into his arms, and I held still, needing to absorb this moment. I cataloged the feel of him, the scent of him. His embrace was always sheltering, always protective. His strength emanated in a subtle vibration. He smelled good, so uniquely him. A laugh bubbled up inside.

He leaned back as I peered up. "What's so funny?" His eyes glinted with mirth, and his smile was warm.

I shrugged. "You're going to think it's silly."

"I doubt it." He stepped back, catching one of my hands and pulling me with him through his doorway into his house.

"I thought you smelled good and was kind of being mushy about it in my head. You smell like evergreen trees and the ocean."

"That's not silly." His gaze coasted over me, leaving a blaze of heat in its wake.

"You tend to smell like sugar and flour, sometimes a little salty because you're in the kitchen a lot. But I still think it's *you*. I'm pretty sure if I closed my eyes, I could find you by scent." As we stared at each other, giddiness rose inside.

"I missed you. Two whole days," he said, the low rumble of his voice setting my nerves alight.

"I'm sorry it took so long. My schedule's been nuts."

He was shaking his head before I even finished talking. "I completely understand. I was just emphasizing my feelings." He squeezed my hand, adding, "Follow me."

The two whole days since I'd had time alone with him were for several reasons. I had legitimately had a busy schedule at work. But I'd also needed time. I'd processed it with my mother, who clearly knew how to keep a secret better than I did. When I teased her about that, she pointed out, "Maybe someday you'll learn. You always did wear your heart on your sleeve. I love that about you. You got it from your father."

Tonight, my mom and Lia were having a movie night with pizza and popcorn. For the first time, I could spend the whole night with Blake, and it wouldn't be a secret.

Still, we would have to take things slow beyond stolen nights together, and I was okay with that. Maybe I knew I was in love with him, but I had to consider Lia and how to incorporate Blake into our lives.

"What are we doing?" I asked Blake as we walked into the kitchen.

"I'm cooking us dinner. And then—" He dropped my hand and glanced over his shoulder. The heat banked in his eyes sent my belly into a spinning slip.

I had wondered if, without the secrecy, the edge of my need for him might soften. Apparently not. It felt sharp, almost biting.

He ordered me to sit at the counter, then checked on something in the oven. It was all I could do not to get up and help. He turned around and smiled at me. "You can help. Not because you need to."

"Oh thank God!" I exclaimed as I stood and rounded the counter. "It's not you. It's just I like to do things. What are you making?"

"I have some halibut in the oven. It should be done in a few minutes. I was about to sauté some vegetables to go with it. What would you like to do?"

Impulsively, I leaned up and kissed him. A moment later, we broke apart, both of us breathless.

Blake stared down at me, his gaze dark. "How hungry are you?"

"Not that hungry."

He stepped away, turning and decisively switching off the oven. It said something that my need was rushing so forcefully that I didn't feel pressed to point out that if we didn't hurry, dinner might be ruined.

All I knew was I needed Blake. I needed the feel of his hands on me. I needed him inside me, to be physically joined with him as completely as I could be

Moments later, our mouths were fused, and we were tearing at each other's clothes. Blake lifted me and carried me into the living room. "I can't make it to the bedroom," he bit out when we broke apart to gulp in air.

Fiery hot minutes later, I straddled him, sinking down over his length, and letting out a whimper at the delicious stretch of him filling me. My body was so ready, so primed for him, and my climax burst through me after a few thrusts when he teased his fingers over my swollen clit.

I felt the heat of his release fill me as my head fell into the curve of his shoulder, and the tremors rippled through me. Maybe a moment later, I lifted my head, and he smoothed my hair away from my cheeks. "I meant to take it slow," he whispered gruffly.

I leaned forward, pressing my lips to his. Straightening, I smiled. "We have time for that later." Just then, my stomach growled, and he grinned.

Chapter Forty-Six

BLAKE

Next summer

Lia looked up at me. "Just hold the net?"

"That's it," I said with a firm nod.

"And the fish are just going to swim right into it?" Lia eyed me skeptically.

Fiona smiled down at her, smoothing her hand over her hair. "If Blake says so, then I think that's what will happen."

Lia gripped the net firmly and marched out into the water. Fiona slid her gaze to mine with a bemused grin. "Obviously, I see people coming in and out of the water with fish in their nets, but this is the wildest thing I've ever seen."

I chuckled. "It's wild and a lot of fun."

I was hoping the fish report I'd seen this morning would be accurate. Dipnetting in Alaska was a tradition for residents and one of my favorite things to do. Before my father passed away, he used to take us every year. We'd been joking about it at a family dinner one night, and Lia had been asking to go ever since. We'd taken a trip to the Kenai River after a visit to Willow Brook.

Adam and Kenan were with us today and already in the water. Rhys and Haven had skipped out because they were still adjusting to life with a baby.

"Are you going out in the water?" Fiona asked.

"Of course. I'll wait. Lia gets the first fish."

Time and nature were on our side. Within ten minutes, Lia called, "Blake!"

Every time Fiona's daughter asked for my help with something, my heart felt so full I thought it might crack wide open. I jogged into the water. We were all dressed in waders because running in and out of the water was necessary for dipnetting.

"Hold tight," I said when I reached her. "I think you can get it yourself."

Her eyes were wide as she looked up at me. "It's heavy!"

"You're holding the net." She had a firm grip, so I wanted to give her the confidence she could do this.

She nodded, her eyes locked to the net where we could see a salmon thrashing. I took a position behind her, so I could reach down and grab the net if she started to lose her grip. She never did, and a minute later, we were standing on the sand looking down at a King salmon.

"Good thing I got a King tag," I said when Kenan stopped beside me.

He glanced down at the fish before looking over at Lia and holding both palms up. "High five."

She was grinning from ear to ear as she slapped her palms to Kenan's. Dipnetting was typically for red or silver salmon runs. But you could get a King tag in the event one happened to swim into your net.

I looked down at her. "Well, it's official."

"What's official?" Fiona asked as she stopped beside us.

"Lia's an Alaskan. She caught a King salmon. I've been dipnetting for years and only got one of those."

By the end of the day, we were all exhausted. With the sun high and bright during a long Alaskan summer day, the beach a cacophony of sounds with seagulls flying above us, children's laughter ringing out, and the enthusiastic exclamations of people when they pulled in a salmon, it was a good day.

I was already planning to ask Fiona to marry me. I was impatient for it. We'd done all the right things, or so I thought. We'd taken our time integrating me into their little family, and things had smoothed out at work. Fiona had pointed out there would be gossip no matter who she dated. The one downside was she insisted I never show affection in front of others at work. I didn't know if anyone other than her cared, but I respected her, so I did as she requested.

I had just picked up her ring yesterday, and it was still in my jacket pocket. I made a decision on the fly. Lia was with Adam and Kenan as they showed her how to gut and clean salmon. It was messy work, but she laughed with them as they worked at the cleaning tables.

Fiona and I were loading the coolers in the truck. After we slid the last one in, I looked down at her as she dragged her sleeve across her face. Her usual tidy ponytail had been no match for the wind, the salt-scoured air, and the busyness of dipnetting. She had sand on her cheeks and wore fish waders with a T-shirt.

"Hey," I said when she moved to turn away.

"What?" She turned back, looking up at me.

My heart kicked against my ribs, and I reached into my pocket, my hands closing around the small ring box. "I love you."

She smiled indulgently. "I love you too."

I was going to do this the right way because she deserved it. I knelt, opening the box. "I didn't plan this today, but it feels like the right place. Will you marry me?"

Fiona's mouth fell open as she stared down at me, her eyes wide. She let out a startled gasp. "Oh my God, oh my God!"

I waited.

"Are you serious?" she pressed.

"Absolutely. I love you, and you're the only person I can imagine spending the rest of my life with."

"Yes," she whispered as tears rolled down her cheeks.

I was sliding the ring on her finger when one of my brothers looked over and called out, "Well, damn."

"You're not supposed to swear," Lia said.

"Some occasions call for it," Adam added.

It was only then that Lia turned and looked over. She squealed, jumping up and down before she ran over to us. Adam wisely snatched the fillet knife out of her hand as she dashed by him.

I hugged her close as I stood and pulled Fiona into my arms.

They were my heart.

Kenan Cannon

"Dude, breathe," I said to my brother.

Blake spun around. "I haven't seen Fiona since last night."

Rhys had already gotten married. He'd been a wreck too. Somehow, I hadn't expected Blake to be the proverbial hot mess about his wedding.

But then, "I should've known," I said, completing my thought aloud.

"Should've known what?" Blake countered as he paced back and forth in the small waiting room.

"That you'd be nervous. You're the coolest customer of all of us, always quick with a joke. But you love Fiona. If only she knew just how whipped you are," I teased.

Blake let out a laugh as he rolled his eyes and finally stopped his pacing. "You're right." He glanced at his watch.

"One more minute."

As if the universe was conspiring to give Blake a break, there was a light knock on the door. Haven peered inside. "Are we ready?

"Oh, he's ready," I replied. "We'd better get this show on the road before he has a legit meltdown in here."

Haven opened the door wider, smiling warmly at Blake. "I love that you're so in love."

Blake shrugged. "I am."

A moment later, we walked outside. It was late summer, and we were having the wedding at the harbor. Fiona and Blake had a favorite bench near a small park to one side of the harbor. I walked beside Blake, taking in the arch with fireweed flowers twined around it. Hazel was presiding over the wedding.

I was Blake's best man. I was surprised Blake didn't kiss Fiona before the vows even got started. She looked stunning in a lovely cream gown with her hair down and fireweed flowers placed artfully in her hair at the request of her daughter. Maybe fireweed wasn't a glamorous flower, but it was beautiful and the namesake for our town.

I watched while another brother pledged his heart. All the while, I couldn't imagine getting married. It definitely wasn't my thing. But then, my two older brothers had been just as cynical as me once upon a time.

After Fiona and Blake exchanged vows, my throat felt tight, and my chest was almost hurting. Their love was the real deal. I hoped it held for them.

Hours later, at the reception at Fireweed Winery, Blake stopped beside me with Fiona's hand firmly in his. "I've probably said it ten times today already, but congratulations," I offered with a grin.

Blake smiled widely, the sheer joy in his face so pure. I'd watched my brother, who used to shield himself with jokes, showing Fiona's daughter how to cut the cake. The clear love on his face was something to see.

He was a true family man, and I was happy for him. Meanwhile, I was feeling even more cynical about life lately. I joked that I was the catchall in my family's business, and I was. I did whatever needed to be done. Usually, I enjoyed that. But lately, I'd been feeling betwixt and between, as if I didn't know where I fit. Watching two brothers get married in the past two years had churned up a sense of uncertainty, and I didn't understand why.

My twin brother, Adam, was the CFO of our family's corporation. Numbers were his strength, and I loathed them. The other set of twins in our family, Wyatt and Griffin, were hotshot firefighters. They loved it. My sister happily ran the public relations arm of our corporation. It just felt like everybody but me knew they had a place. Whether it was in love or in their career, or just how they went about life. Meanwhile, I was the guy who didn't.

I took a breath and gave myself a mental kick. I didn't need to be morose. This wasn't how I went about life. I made my way through the crowd, intending to get another drink. My eyes landed on a small gap in the run of stools surrounding the bar. I slipped over there, murmuring, "Excuse me."

The woman seated there shifted over, saying, "Of course."

Recognizing the voice, I glanced down to see Quinn Blackthorn. She was the lead attorney for our family's corporation and also one of my best friends.

I winked. "Hey, Quinn."

She cleared her throat, her lips curling in

a smile that didn't quite reach her eyes. "Another wedding on the books," she said, lifting her bottle of beer.

As I studied her, an unfamiliar sensation kicked up in my body, the subtle rev of an engine. I'd always known, objectively speaking, that Quinn was beautiful. Maybe it's because she was a lawyer and her sharp intelligence intimidated me even though I'd never admit it, maybe it's because she was a friend, or perhaps it's because I was an idiot, but I never paid that kind of attention to her.

I suddenly couldn't look away from her wide hazel eyes. Her eyebrows arched delicately, and she had high cheekbones. My eyes landed on her mouth. Sweet hell. That expression—a mouth made for sin—came to mind. I'd never thought it, certainly not about Quinn. She was just a friend. Right? But holy hell. That mouth was suddenly all I could notice. She had plump lips with the bottom one a little fuller and a pretty curve in the center of her upper lip.

She cleared her throat, and my eyes snapped up to meet hers again.

"How's it going, Quinn?" I asked, trying to keep my tone casual.

She looked up at me, and when she blinked, I noticed how thick her eyelashes were. What in the ever-loving fuck was happening? I wasn't in the habit of paying attention to eyelashes, much less Quinn's.

She lifted one shoulder in an elegant shrug. "It's going. The wedding was nice," she added with a curl of her lips.

A sizzle of heat zipped down my spine. Although I saw Quinn often and considered her one of my closest friends, I'd never—and I do mean *never*—had this kind of reaction to her.

"Kenan?" she prompted. "You in there?"

"It was," I finally managed.

I glanced over toward Blake and Fiona. Blake looked happy, but more than that, he carried himself with a sense of peace. That was what struck me the most ever since he and Fiona had been together

Looking back toward Quinn, I added, "I'm really happy for them."

She nodded, her eyes lighting up as they shifted to Blake and Fiona and back to me. "They seem really happy. Are you next?"

"Next?"

She cocked her head to the side, arching a brow. "To fall in love and get married. It seems the thing to do in your family these days."

I shook my head swiftly. "I don't think so."

She made a noncommittal sound in her throat, followed by, "Mmm."

"What does that mean?"

"Nothing."

Defensiveness pricked at me. "It seemed like something." Quinn's eyes widened slightly. "I don't think it's possible to really know who will get married and who will stay married," I added.

She rolled her eyes. "I certainly don't plan to get married."

"Makes sense."

Another eye roll. I sensed her discomfort and felt relieved. I didn't need to be the only one feeling off. "Why does it make sense?" she pressed.

"Because you seem married to your job."

Quinn's nostrils flared as she took a breath, and a slight flush crested on her cheeks. Oh, this was fun. I liked getting under her skin.

"I'm *not* married to my job," she ground out.

"Sure seems like it to me. I'm not even at the office all that much, but I have never been there, no matter the time of day, without you being in your office."

"It's my job. If I'm working, it's on something for Fireweed Industries."

"Oh, sure, but you don't have to work all the time," I pointed out.

I sensed I'd hit a sore spot for Quinn. Of course, this was convenient because I didn't like how she had hit a sore spot for me, one I didn't even know I had.

Just then, the bartender paused beside us, flashing a quick grin at us. "Anything for you two?"

"I'll take whatever the limited beer is this week," I replied.

"I'll take the same," Quinn chimed in as she slid her now-empty bottle across the bar.

He nodded, and then a moment later, he glanced up. "There's only one left."

"Just one?" I prompted.

"It's limited for a reason," he teased as he pulled it out and unscrewed the cap. "So who gets it?"

I thumbed toward Quinn. "She does."

"No need," she said with an airy wave. "You go ahead and have it, Kenan."

"No, it's yours," I insisted.

Quinn rolled her eyes and took it. "Thank you."

I ordered another beer, and the bartender

went to get it out of the back. "Wow, you're making him work," she teased.

I looked over at Quinn just as she lifted her bottle to take a swallow. The sight of those plump lips closing around the end of the bottle sent a fiery jolt through me. I looked away quickly, convinced this was all a fluke. It had to be. My eyes landed on Blake and Fiona. He was dancing with her, leaning down to say something to her. The look of love in his gaze was so intimate, I felt as if we were all interrupting a private moment.

When I glanced back toward Quinn, she was studying me in that way she had, her gaze direct and unabashed. I told myself this was a momentary and out-of-character fluke for me. The next time I saw Quinn, she would have her head bowed at her desk while she worked on something. I wouldn't think she had the sexiest mouth I'd ever seen.

Thank you for reading Blake & Fiona's story! Want a glimpse of the future for them? Join my newsletter to receive an exclusive scene.

Sign up here: https://BookHip.com/BLHFLVA

p.s. If you are already subscribed, you'll still be able to access the scene.

Up next in the Fireweed Harbor Series is Be The One.

Kenan and Quinn are best friends. Just friends. That's it.

Until one kiss. One of those earth-shaking, knee-melting, mind-blowing kisses.

Don't miss Kenan & Quinn's smokin' hot, friends to lovers, holiday romance!

Pre-order Be The One - due out Oct 9, 2023!

For more swoony romance...

This Crazy Love kicks off the Swoon Series - small town southern romance with enough heat to melt you! Jackson & Shay's story is epic - swoon-worthy & intensely emotional. Jackson just happens to be Shay's brother's best friend. He's also *seriously* easy on the eyes. Shay has a past, the kind of past she would most definitely like to forget. Past or not, Jackson is about to rock her world. Don't miss their story! Free on all retailers!

Burn For Me is a second chance romance for the ages. Sexy firefighters? Check. Rugged

men? Check. Wrapped up together? Check. Brave the fire in this hot, small-town romance. Amelia & Cade were high school sweethearts & then it all fell apart. When they cross paths again, it's epic - don't miss Cade's story!
Free on all retailers!

For more small town romance, take a visit to Last Frontier Lodge in Diamond Creek. A sexy, alpha SEAL meets his match with a brainy heroine in Take Me Home. Marley is all brains & Gage is all brawn. Sparks fly when their worlds collide. Don't miss Gage & Marley's story!
Free on all retailers!

If sports romance lights your spark, check out The Play. Liam is a British footballer who falls for Olivia, his doctor. A twist of forbidden heats up this swoon-worthy & laugh-out-loud romance. Don't miss Liam & Olivia's story.
Free on all retailers!

5) Follow me on Instagram at https://www.
     instagram.com/jhcroix/
6) Like my Facebook page at https://www.
     facebook.com/jhcroix

———

Visit my store to purchase ebooks & fun swag!
    J.H. Croix Shop
    Fireweed Harbor Series
    Make You Mine
    Dare To Fall
    Be The One - due out Oct 2023!
    Light My Fire Series
    Wild With You
    Hold Me Now
    Only Ever Us
    Fall For Me
    Keep Me Close
    With Every Breath
    All It Takes
    Take Me Now - coming August 2023!
    Dare With Me Series
    Crash Into You
    Evers & Afters
    Come To Me
    Back To Us
    Take Me There

After We Fall

Swoon Series

This Crazy Love

Wait For Me

Break My Fall

Truly Madly Mine

Still Go Crazy

If We Dare

Steal My Heart

Into The Fire Series

Burn For Me

Slow Burn

Burn So Bad

Hot Mess

Burn So Good

Sweet Fire

Play With Fire

Melt With You

Burn For You

Crash & Burn

That Snowy Night

Brit Boys Sports Romance

The Play

Big Win

Out Of Bounds

Play Me

Naughty Wish

Diamond Creek Alaska Novels

When Love Comes

Follow Love
Love Unbroken
Love Untamed
Tumble Into Love
Christmas Nights

Last Frontier Lodge Novels

Take Me Home
Love at Last
Just This Once
Falling Fast
Stay With Me
When We Fall
Hold Me Close
Crazy For You
Just Us

ACKNOWLEDGMENTS

Readers! Thank you, thank you, thank you!

Much appreciation to my editor who helped me give Fiona & Blake the love story they deserve, and to my proofreader who scours for the details and tidies up those pesky timelines. Gracious thanks to my early readers who find the stubborn errors.

Najla Qamber created another stunning cover for this story. Much love to the bloggers, bookstagrammers, and booktokers who share their love of stories with the rest of the world.

Thank you and then some to my assistant, Erin, for helping me with *so* many details.

To DBC and our dogs. All the love.

xoxo
J.H. Croix